I0549398

A Plain Man's Talk on the Labor Question

Simon Newcomb

Contents

A PLAIN MAN'S TALK ON THE LABOR QUESTION

BY

Simon Newcomb

A PLAIN MAN'S TALK ON
THE LABOR QUESTION

PREFACE.

The following chapters owe their inception to the editor of the New York Independent in which journal the outlines of most of them have recently appeared. They are now recast, amplified, and submitted to the courteous consideration of the reader.

PART I SOCIETY AND ITS WANTS
A PLAIN MAN'S TALK ON THE LABOR QUESTION.

I.
TO THE READER.

I Do not address you, dear reader, as an authority on this subject, propounding a code of doctrine which you are bound to accept. I am only a plain man, who has all his life tried to find out what he could, from study and observation, about the state of society in different countries of the world, and about the relation between the great operations of industry and commerce on the one side, and human welfare on the other. I do not expect to tell you anything which you cannot easily understand, and most of the facts I have to lay before you you must already know; or, atleast, you can easily verify. Of doctrine I have little, and of theory still less.

Indeed, I am not a believer in any rigid theory of society, for the simple reason that any theory we may propound is liable to be modified by changes in the condition of society. The way I look at the labor question is this:

We find ourselves face to face with a state of things which no thinking person can contemplate without deep solicitude. Wide-spread dissatisfaction prevails among the laboring classes, not only in this country, but in the most enlightened countries of Europe. What gives gravity to the problem is, that these classes wield a power, social and political, which they never before wielded in the world's history. Their power is reinforced by a belief among the intellectual classes, and in society generally, that men have accumulated large fortunes by unworthy means, and that great corporations exert a power for evil which society ought not to tolerate. When we inquire how it is that great fortunes have been gained and dangerous powers acquired by compact bodies of men, we find it to be in pursuance of a certain way of doing business which we have inherited from our ancestors, and of which the main feature is founded on the supposed right of every man to get as rich as he can by lawful combinations and bargains with his fellow-men, and to use the wealth thus acquired in the way that he thinks best. The question whether this system will, and ought to be, permanent, or whether it is unsuited to the new conditions of production which now prevail, is the great question of the day.

We see everywhere in society a deep-seated belief that there is something wrong in a state of society in which one man may be enormously rich while another has not a place that he can call his own in which to lay his head. The great object of the labor movement is to do something towards curing the wrong. Every right-feeling man must sympathize with this object because every such person must desire the good of all his fellow-men.

But it does not follow that, because labor-organizations desire to cure the evil, therefore all the measures they propose will have that effect. Suppose all their measures well adapted to getting out of the frying-pan, the proverb tells us where they may then find themselves. The interests of sixty millions of people make a very complicated whole, which the mind cannot easily grasp; and when we try to promote them at one point, we may set them back at a hundred other points without knowing it. The only way to reach a satisfactory conclusion is, to study out all the facts of the case, beginning with the biggest ones, and going step by step to those which are smaller. Great and universal facts should form the basis of all our thought upon the subject, because they are of vastly more importance than the special facts, which, by their newness and force, strike our attention at the moment.

In accordance with this general method of viewing the subject, I have tried to see what is the greatest fact with which we have to deal, and I find it to be the one which forms the title of the following chapter.

II. SOCIETY IS A CO-OPERATIVE UNION.

THE first and greatest fact we have to deal with is, that the society of which we are all members has grown into a great co-operative association, extending over the whole country, nay, over the civilized world. Look where we will, we find that every one is working for the good of people whom, in most cases, he never saw and never expects to see. For example: walking through the streets of a city we find hodcarriers and bricklayers engaged in erecting a building. But not one of the men at work on that building will ever live in it. Yet it will be sure to benefit some one. If it is a warehouse, it will, perhaps, be used for the storage of clothing for thousands of other people; possibly for people who are not yet born. If a dwelling, a family, or a score of families, will soon be sheltered by it. Going a little farther, we see a cobbler at work. He is mending shoes for his neighbor." A little farther on we find a furniture factory. Here a thousand men are running machinery to make furniture for their fellow-men. The chairs they make may be used in half the states of the Union. Going through the streets where retail stores are situated we shall find merchants and clerks taking care of and selling goods for all the people of the city. If we go into a manufacturing town we shall find operatives weaving cloth or forging iron for the community. If we watch a railway we shall find that the thousand men engaged in funning it are bringing goods for the use of the people of a whole city, or of a whole state.

Moreover, everything that all these people are doing is for the benefit of others. Let us in imagination walk along a railway and stop the first freight train that comes along. We insist on finding out what interest we have in that freight train. Opening the first car, we find it loaded with hides, which are to be tanned into leather, which leather is to be made into boots and shoes. Accidents aside, every hide will help to clothe somebody's feet. Another car we find loaded with flour. Every pound of that flour is going to be eaten by somebody; and what the men in charge of it are now doing is to bring it within the reach of the consumer. Another car we find loaded with butter and apples. Every pound of that butter and every one of those apples are to be eaten by somebody. Go in this way through the whole list, and examine every car on every railway in the country, and you will find that each is loaded with something for somebody, and that all the work of the men running the railway is for the benefit of the people who are finally to make use of the goods they are transporting.

As you read these lines there are tens of thousands of men scattered from Maine to California—nay, spread over the various countries of Europe and Asia—who are at work on things which are to minister to your individual well-being, one, two, or three years hence. Men in China are raising tea, which is to supply you with drink. Men in France are raising sheep, the wool off of whose backs will go into your future coat. A man in Dakota is cutting a log, the timber of which will go into a match with which you are to light your candle. A cowboy in Texas is now pasturing the animal out of whose hide the boots you are to wear two years hence will be made. A man in Cornwall is digging out tin ore, the metal from which will go upon the roof of your house to protect you from the rain. Men in Scotland are building a ship which will bring the tin over to you. Men in Philadelphia are preparing the machinery for rolling the iron on which the tin will be spread. Men in Illinois are preparing the ground to raise the wheat to make the bread which you will eat during the next two years.

I have studied a great many things, both in the heavens and on the earth, but nowhere have I found anything more marvellous than this social organism, a glimpse of whose operations I have tried to give you. The most marvellous thing about it is that the operations are all carried on by men who seem to their fellows entirely selfish. We cannot possibly claim that all these thousands of people who are at work providing for your comfort during the next two, three, or four years are actuated by love for you. Following out the principles which I have laid down, we need not inquire too closely into their motives. The great fact is that they are working for our benefit; and so long as they do this we need not criticise their motives.

Let it satisfy us to remember that "handsome is as handsome does."

I feel that my description of this social machine is extremely inadequate; but the reader knows as much about it as I do, and must complete the description for himself. I beg that he will look around his room and his house, think what he is going to eat and drink during the next few years, and try in imagination to picture to himself the present activities of the men on whose industry his future happiness depends. If he will thus get a complete picture of the facts as he already knows them well in his mind, he will have the key to the whole problem of the labor question.

I now have to make an application of the great fact just set forth. The question is often raised whether men are born under a natural obligation to use their powers and faculties for the benefit of their fellows. I am disposed to hold that they are. But the question has always seemed to me, at its best, a somewhat barren one, for the simple reason that it is idle for us to claim the validity of any such obligation unless we can enforce it. Laws which cannot be enforced do more harm than good whether in morals or politics. But the point which I wish now to urge is, that the interest which might attach to this question of moral obligation is diminished by the great fact that men are already engaged in using their best faculties for each other's benefit. We really have, among us and around us, the very Utopia which social philosophers have so often dreamed of; a state of society in which, if not every man, at least a large majority of men, are using their best faculties for everybody else's benefit. When they stop doing this—when the physician refuses to heal, the railway manager to direct, the Congressman to legislate, the professor to teach, the actor to go upon the stage, the farmer to sow and reap, the engine-driver to run his engine, the carpenter to build, the bricklayer to do his work, and the grocer to sell his goods—then we shall have before us the great, burning question whether we are all to compel each other to perform our social obligations. So far as the present juncture is concerned, all I can say is that the views set forth in this little book will be found in perfect consistency with the theory that man is born with some obligations towards his fellow-man, but that I see no present need of urging the theory. The real point on which men differ is, not the question of obligation, but the question what a man ought to do if he wanted to fulfil the obligation, and this is the question I want to submit to your judgment.

At this point I have a confession to make. It has seemed to me that, in nearly all practical and social questions, the true position was that of the golden mean. But on this particular subject of the social organization I must confess that I am an ultraist, in admiring the co-operative system at work among us. When I reflect that two hundred years ago nearly all our ancestors went barefoot, because only a few rich people could supply their children with shoes; that a hundred years ago none except the rich had any clothes except what they made themselves, nor any food except what they raised by their own labor; and when I now look and see railway managers planning and thinking how they can so manage their trains as to bring to you, to me, and to our families, in the quickest and surest way, the fruit from California which we so like to eat, the butter from New York State, the hides from Texas, and the flour from Chicago, which are so necessary to our comfort— I say when, in addition to all these thousands of men who are making these things for us, we see these great administrators of railways patiently planning by day and night the most effective way to supply our wants—I am astonished that any man should be otherwise than most thankful that he was not born until the nineteenth century. If the reader thinks he could devise any better system for his own happiness or for that of his neighbor he has a much higher opinion of his own ability than I have of mine. I confess that I should despair of inventing any system under which that man up in Dakota should be insured to cut down the timber to get the wood to make the matches to light my gas with next year, and to secure the proper co-operation among all the thousands of men who must work on those matches, both in making and transporting them, until the grocer's boy in his wagon shall deliver them at my door. If you, dear reader, have any plan by which this will all be done more economically than it is done now, by which you can guarantee that all the cutters of timber, the makers of rafts, the men in the sawmill, the brakemen on the railway, the manufacturers of chlorate of potash, the diggers of sulphur, the makers of machinery, the makers of match-boxes, the grocers and the grocer's boy, shall every one perform his functions without fail, I should like to know it. But I do not think you have.

Possibly, however, you think there are certain unsatisfactory features in its workings which you could remedy if you had the power No doubt there are. No matter how well a thing may be done, we always find it to admit of improvement. Much as I admire our social system, I know it has many imperfections. My main object in preparing these talks is to see what causes of complaint we have, and whether we can heal them better than they will heal themselves. What we most want to know at the present critical juncture is whether the policy urged by friends of the labor movement will make the laborer better or worse off; hence we have to consider the interests of the laborer as well as of every one else.

III.
OUR COMMON INTERESTS.

FROM the facts laid down in the two preceding chapters we may draw certain inferences of prime importance. Our first inference is that the material welfare of every individual depends entirely upon how much work his fellow-men do to supply his wants. If we consider the products on which our well-being depends—the food we eat, the clothes we wear, the beds we sleep upon, and the houses which shelter us, we find that they are all results of the labor of other men. Moreover, so far as merely material prosperity is concerned, that is, the prosperity for which we are all laboring, our welfare depends wholly upon the extent to which we can get our fellow-men to supply our wants. No matter how dull business may be, no matter how little money we may have, no matter how low our wages, if we are only assured for ourselves and our children that we shall be warmly and comfortably clothed, housed, and supplied with all requisite nourishment, bodily and mental, then we are prosperous. Thus our prosperity depends upon what we get our fellow-men to do for us, and upon nothing else.

Of course it is not claimed that this kind of prosperity is the only kind worth having. Strong digestion and a good conscience are more important than better food and finer clothes; but we cannot buy these great requisites from anybody. I am here talking only of things made for us by our fellow-men, and which we cannot make for ourselves.

I now wish to illustrate the great fact that the general prosperity and welfare of the community at large, so far as they arise from material things outside of ourselves, depend upon the quantity of things that are produced by human labor, and upon nothing else. Let us begin with the need of houses, and let us see how completely the satisfaction of that need depends upon the number of houses that can be built.

There are, we may suppose, sixty millions of people now living within the limits of the United States. Let us suppose that there are in all four millions of houses within the same limits. Then it is mathematically certain that, on the average, we must put fifteen people into each house. By no kind of legislation, by no organization, by no social changes, can we get sixty millions of people into four millions of houses without putting an average of fifteen into each house. If this is a greater number than the average house will conveniently hold, then it is mathematically certain that the inconvenience can be relieved only by building more houses, and that the greater the number of houses built, the more rapidly the means of relief will be attained. Thus our whole sixty millions of people, no matter what their occupations—capitalists, laborers, carpenters, bricklayers, and farmers—have a deep interest in getting as many houses built as possible, and every kind of action on the part of house-builders which diminishes the number of houses built tends to the discomfort of everybody.

Another consideration may be adduced. During the next ten years the population will probably increase by fifteen millions. If we adopt the principle that every fifteen persons must have a house, then a million of new houses must be built during that time to keep up our present degree of comfort, and we must also keep the present ones in repair. There is, therefore, a still greater necessity that we shall get as many houses built as possible. Thus we see clearly that if bricklayers, carpenters, plasterers, lumbermen, and others whose services are necessary to build houses insist on reducing their hours of labor by twenty-five per cent., the whole community will, with mathematical certainty, be subjected to a certain amount of physical discomfort for want of the house-room to which they are accustomed. I say this is a physical and mathematical necessity, from which no adjustment of wages and no public policy will relieve us. What we have said of the necessity of houses is true of everything else conducive to our comfort and our subsistence. If we divide the number of barrels of flour produced in the country by the number of families in it, we shall have the average number of barrels which each family may possibly have. To find the average which each family really gets we must, of course, subtract the number sent abroad before we make the division. It is then certain that we shall have a certain quantity which cannot be exceeded for the average use of each family. If the sum total of flour produced is diminished by any cause whatever, there will be less to eat. Moreover, since all flour produced is finally eaten, the greater the crops the more flour everybody will have.

Again, in the case of clothes, every suit of clothes which is made is worn by somebody, and none can be worn by anybody unless they are first made, Hence we all have an interest in having managers of factories, tailors, leather-makers, shoemakers, and a host of other people engaged in promoting the manufacture of clothing and shoes, working as long and efficiently as possible.

Of course, if any of these things which are now made by human labor hereafter be made by machinery, so as to save labor, we shall be the better off. A certain amount of labor will be set free from the manufacture which can be employed either in improving the product, or in making something else which we want. If we reflect how utterly inadequate all the labor of the country would have been to produce a quarter of the good things which surround us, had labor-saving machinery never been introduced, we shall see how much we all owe to this machinery.

We also see that there can be no great destruction of property, no matter to whom it belongs, without damaging thousands or millions of people to greater or less degree. No doubt when the unthinking man reads of such a great calamity as that of the great Chicago fire in 1871, he feels sorry for it only because others suffered; and he thinks he did not suffer himself at all. Yet, on the average, the people of the country at large were the worse off for that fire. Of course, the calamity most affected the hundred thousand people who were for a time rendered houseless, and who had to suffer privations while houses were being built; but the wheat that was burned diminished the quantity that was available for the country at large, and increased the price in the same proportion. Thousands all over the country had, during the year or two following, to go with a little less bread than they would otherwise have had.

There is a way of thinking of those conclusions which will greatly help the reader to judge whether any particular policy does or does not benefit the public at large. The annual products of the country form a certain sum total which, if we knew what they were, we could add up at the end of each year. For example, at the end of each year there will be a certain number of houses finished, a certain number of barrels of flour produced, a certain number of suits of clothes made, and so on. We may imagine all these things to be brought into one great central depository. Then we may imagine everybody who uses them to take them out of the depository. We then see that nobody should be allowed to take anything out unless he puts an equivalent in. We also see that the more put in, the more can be taken out, and vice versa. We shall also see that the question whether the effect of any policy is good or bad depends very largely upon whether it increases or diminishes the sum total of the products necessary for human welfare.

This way of looking at our welfare and prosperity may seem so singular to you as to cause doubt in your own minds of its correctness, I do not ask you to accept it on my authority, but I do ask you to think it over. The common method is to talk about wages, prices, demand for labor, the brisk or dull state of business, the plenty or scarcity of money, and so on. But a very little thought will show you that our real welfare does not consist in any of these things. It may, indeed, be affected by it, but the effect must depend on whether demand for labor, brisk business, plenty of money, competition, combination, and so on, result in our getting more or better food, clothing, houses, and furniture. I think, therefore, the true way is to go right down to the actual things we want and see what will help us to get them. Instead of thinking of these indirect agencies, as we are prone to do, let us think of the things themselves—food, clothing, and shelter. If you do this, you will clearly see that it is for your interest and mine that all the things necessary to supply our wants are made and brought within our reach, and that, if this is assured, we need not care further for the state of the market.

IV.
OBJECTIONS CONSIDERED.

EVERY person capable of reasoning must see that the conclusions that I have drawn are unavoidable, so far as the general or average prosperity is concerned. But the question may arise in the mind of the reader whether increasing the general prosperity in the way pointed out necessarily increases the prosperity of each individual. I can imagine him to make the following reply to all I have been saying on the subject:

"You show plainly enough that if we put sixty millions of men into four millions of houses, we must, on the average, put fifteen people into each house; and I readily admit that, were one million of new houses built, we should, on the average, have to put only twelve people into each house. What you call the average prosperity, obtained by dividing the number of people by the number of houses, will no doubt be thus improved. But it does not at all follow that there will be any proportional increase in the actual material prosperity of the people, as you yourself have defined it. As a matter of fact, although the people may average fifteen to a house, they are divided very unequally. Some large houses have only a single family, of perhaps five people, all told. In our great cities there are large tenement houses in which hundreds live in a single house. Now if the million new houses built were all to be occupied by those who now live in crowded quarters, your conclusion would be all right. But would not these new houses, as a matter of fact, be mostly occupied by well-to-do owners, who already have house-room enough, thus leaving the crowded poor as badly off as ever? And so with the bread, the shoes, the clothing, the furniture, and everything else you have described. Who will be benefited if their production is increased? It is not merely a question of producing what the people want, but it is a question of the product going to those who most want it and most deserve it—that is, the laboring classes. How will your theory stand this test?"

I have stated this objection as fairly and strongly as I can, because, as a matter of fact, the thing actually works just the way you think it ought to work. As a general rule, an increase of product is mainly beneficial— not perhaps to the lowest class of all, but certainly to the class of honest skilled and unskilled laborers. Let us look closely into the question. A million new houses are built. As things go, will those houses be occupied principally by the rich, who already have house-room enough, or by those classes who have not house-room enough, or will it be divided between them? I reply to this that they will be mainly occupied by those who most need houses, and who are industrious enough to pay rent for them, and that very few will be taken by the rich. The reason of this is that the rich have already all the house-room that they want, and will have it, do what we will. Practically they have the first pick out of the depository we imagined in the last chapter, and so will take out just what they want, and no more. So what is added is not for their benefit, but for the benefit of those who are less fortunate. For example, a rich man with his family cannot occupy more than one house, except in rare instances, where a man of wealth keeps several for his own benefit. The number who want to do this is so very small that if a million additional houses were built we may be assured that not one out of fifty of them would be occupied by those who are rich enough to have all the house-room they want. They might indeed vacate old houses to occupy the new ones, but then the old ones would be for rent, just as if they had been newly built. The additional million of houses would therefore be mostly occupied by those who now have need of more house-room for their own comfort.

It may be still further asked how the laboring classes could have more house-room unless they were better able to pay house rent? This question is answered very simply and briefly by saying that the increased number of houses would result in the lowering of rents. The owner of each house of course wants to get some benefit out of it, and, if he cannot live in it himself, the only possible way by which he can be benefited is in getting somebody else to live in it and pay rent for it. Hence house-owners would be obliged to lower their rents until they got tenants. Moreover, we must remember that in designing and building a house, their own interest would lead them to keep in view the wants of the particular classes who would be able to rent new houses when the rents were a little lower.

What we have said of houses is yet more true of the other necessities of life. Suppose a diminution in the production of beef and pork brought about by a strike on the part of laborers engaged in producing the staples of life. It is then mathematically certain that the community, taken as a whole, will have less beef and pork to eat. Does the objector think that in this case it will be the rich rather than the poor who suffer? If he does, he thinks the contrary to the truth. The Vanderbilts and the Goulds have no regard to the scarcity or the high price of food in deciding what and how much they shall eat. They never said to their wives, "Beef is so high we must stop eating it and take to pork." "Pork is so high that we must economize in its use." "Flour is so dear the children must be satisfied with corn-cake." But since, when the supply is diminished, it is mathematically certain that somebody will have to have less beef and pork to eat, if this somebody is not among the rich, he will be found elsewhere. Hence it will not be the rich, but the poor, who, finding the price raised, will be compelled to economize. Thus the whole pressure will fall upon the poor.

The very same thing is true of clothing. No matter how much the production of clothing may be diminished, the wealthy will get all the clothes they want. They will wear them so long as they are fashionable, and then they will give or sell them to poorer people. The man who must wear an old coat a week longer in consequence of a scarcity will not be a rich man, but a poor one. We thus see that the objection, instead of operating against the theory we have laid down, operates to strengthen it, by showing that it is the laboring classes who have the greatest interest in the manufacture of the necessaries of life, and in the continuous running of the railway trains and other machinery of communication necessary to bring the products to those who want them.

The objector may claim that all this does not quite cover the point he wishes to make. Perhaps he proceeds as follows:

"What you admit about the advantages which the rich have over the poor is one of the very things I complain of. You say that society actually is a great co-operative union. I grant it. But it is a union which does not divide its profits fairly among its members. It gives one man a hundred or a thousand times what it does another; and there is no such difference as that among their merits. Our system does not lead to justice in the distribution of the products of labor. Tour claim that if we improve our work by building more houses, and producing more abundantly of the necessaries of life, the poor will get most of the advantage, does not do away with this fundamental injustice."

Desiring, as I do, to make no claims which the reader will not consider valid, I must say that I cannot fully answer this objection in the present chapter. In fact, the remaining part of the present book is principally devoted to answering it, directly or indirectly. I cannot even claim that a conclusive answer is possible, for the simple reason that questions of justice are very largely questions between a man and his own conscience. I shall endeavor to anticipate your verdict only by suggesting two points.

In the first place, I hope to show to your entire satisfaction that the proportion of injustice to justice is far less than is generally supposed, and that there is no such inequality in the general distribution of the products of labor as men think there is. True, the inequalities are great, very great, but I think that, looking at them on a large scale, you will find that they are not inconsistent with Christian justice and the well-being of the race.

In the next place, I must point out that the practical side of the question is that on which it must finally turn. Granting that things are not exactly what they ought to be, that is no reason for changing them by making them worse. I am in hearty sympathy with every effort to make them better; and I do not believe there is any difference of opinion between the reader and myself as to what a better state of things would consist in. We fully agree that things will be improved when every man can earn a comfortable living without laboring more hours a day than is good for his health and happiness. The only point on which we can differ is whether particular measures, especially those proposed by labor organizations, are going to promote this object or retard it. Now this is the very question that I have written this little book to discuss, so that we need not consider the matter further in this chapter.

There is still another objection which possibly might have been the first one to present itself to the mind of the reader. He will probably put it in the following shape:

"You seem to think that human welfare is necessarily promoted by always increasing the quantity of the necessaries of life produced. You forget that after enough of these necessaries to supply the wants of the population is produced it is a waste of labor and a positive disadvantage to produce more. For example: when we have made all the clothes that people want to wear, nobody will be the better off for piling up more clothing in warehouses. The same is true of all the necessaries of life —food, clothing and shelter. The overproduction of the necessaries of life is not only useless, but it is a positive disadvantage, because it lowers their price, and thus tends to lower the wages of those engaged in the production." This objection would arise from mistaking my meaning. When I talk of increasing the production of those things necessary to our welfare, I do not mean making the same old goods in greater quantity, but making them of better quality and making new and better kinds of goods. For example: suppose that the labor of all the clothiers and tailors of the country sufficed to keep the population comfortably clad. Then suppose that au improvement in producing clothes is made of such a kind that the whole population could be clad in the same way by the labor of one half of those clothiers and tailors. The whole body of the latter could then make twice as much clothing of the same kind. But they will not do this, nor do I mean that they ought to do it. What they really ought to do, and what they will do, is to employ the labor saved by the improvement in making the clothes finer, softer, warmer, and better; in putting more needlework into the dresses of your children, so that they shall look nice when they go upon the street; in making you white table-cloths, so that you will have a nicer looking table to give you an appetite for your dinner; in making cushions for your chairs, and better beds to sleep on, and so forth. It is surprising how soon you will find yourself able to enjoy twice the product when it takes these improved forms. This is the kind of improvement that has been going on for the past hundred years, and is likely to go on for a hundred years to come.

If it is not perfectly clear to you that honest, efficient workingmen are those who have gained the most by machinery, manufactures, and railways, then you have only to learn from your grandparents what wages your predecessors used to command fifty years ago, what kind of beds they used to sleep on, what kind of chairs they used to sit on, and so forth. Find out, also, how often they could afford a doctor, and what kind of schooling the children got. If you will do this carefully, and read in Professor McMaster's "History of the United States" how these things were a hundred years ago, I have no fear of the result.

V.
BENEFITS AND EVILS OF ORGANIZED ACTION.

WE ought all to feel greatly interested in the question: What measures promote the public good, and what measures retard it? Every man is a part of society, and whatever is for the good of society at large will promote his interest, while whatever injures society injures every member of it. Hence, whenever we hear of a public movement of any kind, an eight-hour movement, a great strike, a rise in prices, a tariff law, a boycott, the first question we should ask is: Will that movement tend to the benefit or to the injury of society at large?

Now, the great advantage of the way of looking at our common interests which I have pointed out in the preceding chapters is, that it affords us a rule for answering this great question in nearly every case which arises.

Every kind of action which gives the public at large a better supply of the necessaries and comforts of life promotes our prosperity; everything which diminishes that supply retards our prosperity. We have, therefore, only to inquire whether more or less service is rendered the public by any course of action to judge of the effects of that action.

As a general rule, every man promotes his own interest when he takes such measures that he can render better service to the public. For, as a general rule, he will be able to command a higher price for that better service. Then he benefits the public and himself at the same time.

But he may also benefit himself by such a course of action that the public shall be in greater need of his services, so that he shall be able to exact a higher price without improving those services. Such a policy will, as a general rule, injure the public more than it will benefit him. Assuming, as I do, that the reader feels an interest in the public welfare, and wants to know whether any particular policy does or does not promote that welfare, I will give some illustrations of the principle just laid down.

When the members of a medical society direct their efforts towards learning how to cure disease by exchanging the results of their own experience and study, they promote the public good, because they thus learn how to treat diseases more effectively, and to heal their patients more rapidly. It is to their own profit to do this, because the better healers of disease they can make themselves, the more ready their patients will be to employ them. But when they combine by an agreement that they will not visit a patient for less than a certain fixed price, their action tends to the public injury, because they may exclude many poor patients who, not being able easily to pay the price, will go without medical attendance. They injure the public even more than they benefit themselves.

When manufacturers associate themselves together to collect information for improving their methods of producing goods, they benefit the public by giving it a larger supply of the goods. But when they agree that they will not sell below a certain price, even if they have to diminish the supply of goods, then they injure the public, because they gain their end only by increasing the public necessities through cutting off its supplies.

When an association of merchants, or a mercantile exchange, devotes itself to procuring the latest and most exact news of prices and markets in various parts of the world, it promotes the public good, because its members will then buy from the people who most want to sell; and they will sell to the people who are in greatest need of goods, because it is such people who, other conditions being equal, will be willing to pay the highest prices. But if they should combine not to sell below a certain price, and to stop trading unless they could make a certain profit, it would tend to the general injury by lessening the supplies of the necessaries of life.

Please notice the principle involved in all the preceding cases. The whole question turns on whether you attract men to do what you want them to do, or throw obstacles in the way of their doing differently from what you desire. Suppose that you are accustomed to go by a certain road to market. I open a different road, which it is for my advantage that you should take rather than your old road. If I induce you to change by digging up your old road, so that it is harder than before for your horses, and thus press you to take mine, then I injure you. But if I plant my new road with flowers and make it smoother and better than the old one, so that you take it of your own choice, then I benefit you. The distinction between inducing the public and pressing it is so simple that I do not see how any one can fail to see it, yet the astonishing fact is that they do fail. We continually hear people say they are forced to do things which they need not do at all unless it is for their own advantage; and we also hear of applying force or pressure to people in order to give them liberty to do as they please.

This same principle can be applied to the effects of labor organizations. A union of laborers throughout the country, having for its object to get information of the rate of wages in all employments in different parts of the country, and to learn the prices of the necessaries of life with a view of knowing where to apply for work, would be beneficial both to the members and the public. It would benefit the members by enabling them to find the best market for their labor, and it would benefit the public by sending laborers where wages are highest; that is, where the public had most need of labor.

So, also, if the organization devote itself to the improvement of its members in the efficiency with which they could carry on their trade, it would be a public benefit. For example, if an association of carpenters should learn, by comparing notes, how to do ten per cent. more work in the same time, and still do it in the very best manner, it would be a public benefit, because then each person who lives in a house would be able to have a little larger or better house than he had before the carpenters thus improved themselves. The same thing would be true if bricklayers taught each other how to build a better wall in the same time, or plasterers to do fine and strong work as easily as they now do poor work. In all such cases the wants of the community would be better supplied.

So, also, if a labor union should devote its energies to searching out the idle children of the poor, who are growing up without either manual training or an education, and should induce or encourage all of them to learn such trades as would make them useful members of society, then a great good would be done. I do not know any feature of our modern society more discouraging to the philanthropist than the number of children in our great cities who are growing up with no thought of how they shall earn a living in the future, and I know of no more worthy form of benevolent effort than that directed to their training.

But when such a union agrees that none of its members shall work for less than a certain rate of wages, and makes them stop work because they cannot command these wages, then it injures the public. For every day that its members stop work there will be fewer houses for ourselves and our children. If, by holding out, they finally succeed in commanding the increased wages, they have still suffered privations during their strike, and have gained their end only by increasing the public necessities for their work.

I do not pretend to know authoritatively in which of these two directions labor organizations have tended; but all I have heard of them is in the second direction rather than in the first. I have seldom, if ever, heard of their combining to render better service to the public. Such of their rules as I have seen are rather in the direction of rendering as little service to the community as they conveniently can. For example, it is certain that a man who works ten hours a day will render more service to the community than one who works only eight. But some labor organizations, instead of encouraging their members to work ten hours, fine them if they do it; that is, they seek to compel each other to render a less service to the public.

My object in writing this book is not so much to criticise as to enable other people to criticise and judge for themselves; and, therefore, I shall for the present leave the reader to draw his own conclusions as to what is good and what evil in labor organizations. I may, however, remark that I could never feel quite satisfied of the soundness of the oft-repeated claim that organized labor, as it is called, has been of great benefit to the laborer. I have already shown in part, and shall try to show more fully hereafter, that the enormous increase in the production of the necessaries of life which has resulted from the introduction of machinery could not but make a great improvement in the condition of the laboring classes; and I think that this, and not organization, is the source of the improvement which we have witnessed. But this is a subject to be discussed hereafter.

PART II. CAPITAL AND ITS USES

VI
THE RAILWAY QUESTION: ITS BIG SIDE.

I VERY much fear that I am now going so to expose my ignorance and lack of understanding that the reader will distrust my teachings. But as I promised in setting out only to tell things which the reader as well as myself would understand, I am bound, when I come to something I do not understand, to make a frank confession. I read a great deal in the newspapers, and hear a great deal elsewhere, about the despotic dominion of railway corporations and the grinding monopoly of railways. I confess that I find it quite impossible to understand this view, or to see any reason in it. I have travelled over numerous railways in nearly every quarter of Europe and America, and have been surprised at the pains always taken by their managers to consult my wishes and convenience. Their trains always started at the hour most convenient for me and for my fellows who had to travel over the road. The study and experiments of scores of scientific men, and the mechanical ingenuity of hundreds of inventors, had been drawn upon by the railway managers to make an engine and car which should carry me with great speed in entire safety, and land me at my destination in time to transact my business. Different railway managers had consulted together to have their trains so connect that I should get through with the least possible loss of time. Every man on the road, especially the engine-driver, the most important of all, did his very best to further my objects. Among the men for whom I have a particular admiration are managers of railways and locomotive engineers. When I leave a train I am in the habit of turning my head as I pass the engine to have a good look at the engine-driver who has rendered me so excellent a service and kept such a sharp lookout against any accident happening to me. It seems to me that there is hardly any class of men who show such nerve and such skill, and who have oftener risked or laid down their lives to save their passengers.

The cheapness with which the whole thing is done is one of its marvels. Fifty years ago it would have, been quite incredible that these monopolists should have carried a passenger at the rate of forty or fifty miles an hour at the rate of two cents a mile. Here I may so far anticipate as to remark upon the very small fraction of my money which goes into the pocket of the owners of railways. Much the larger portion is paid out to the thousands of workmen whose services are necessary to my journey.

Where does the grinding and oppression come in? I am sure it is not on the railway. Is it when I am away from the railway? No; I never knew a railway official to follow me after I left the station. Never in Europe or America did one of them come to me and insist that I should ride on his railway. I believe in one or two cases during my life they woke me up by a steam-whistle when I happened to sleep in a hotel near the road. With this exception I was never disturbed by one of these monopolists unless I went to ride on his train, and then I found him doing all he could to carry me to my journey's end in the most easy and convenient way.

Possibly, in my ignorance of this whole subject of monopoly, I have made a great mistake in concluding that it is the public at large which is injured by it. When one is ignorant he has to grasp at mere possibilities; and it may be that it is only the workmen on the railway who are supposed to be injured by the monopoly. If this is so, I confess to an almost equal difficulty in understanding the case. If these railway managers ever force men to run their trains who do not want to do so for the wages they were receiving. I never heard of it. This is a free country, and under our laws not even a Vanderbilt or a Gould can force a man to run their trains one hour longer than he wants to. Where, then, does the injury come in?

I do not deny that a man may temporarily feel himself oppressed by some action of the railway by which he is employed; that a great many arrangements for his comfort and convenience may be omitted; and very little regard paid to his daily wants. If so, he has a perfect right to do all he can to make his complaints heard, and even to leave the service of the road if they remain unheeded. Certainly, it seems to me for the selfish interest of railway managers that they should do the very best they can to please the men, because, the better they treat their men, the more willing the latter will be to serve them, and the less likely to engage in strikes. If, then, they wilfully ill-treat their employees, they are not such sharp men as we commonly suppose, and should rather be classified as dull fools. It seems to me that the general principle that those corporations which treat their men best will get the best service affords about as good a guarantee against ill-treatment as we can well advise. This, however, is a subject on which I am open to correction; indeed, as I have already explained, this whole chapter is little more than a confession of ignorance and lack of understanding, which I should be much obliged to have remedied.

Possibly those who know more may reply that I entirely misunderstand the matter in dispute. The real cause of the complaint may be, not that these railways do not serve the public in the best way they can, but that they are owned and managed by a very hateful, selfish, proud, overbearing set of men, who have managed to accumulate from one million to two hundred millions of dollars each. If this is the case, I immediately raise the question of common-sense as against sentiment.

I say boldly that I do not care how selfish, proud, wicked, and overbearing the managers and owners of these roads may be, nor do I care if they own one million or one thousand million dollars, if they only arrange their trains to suit my convenience and convey me at the lowest rates. What should we think of a man who brought such sentimental: considerations into his practical, every-day life? Suppose, for example, that a man should refuse to have an ivory ornament or utensil because the elephant from which it came was a very large and ugly animal, who had trampled a man to death? What should we think if he would not allow his children to learn geography because the geographies tell us about the Atlantic Ocean, which has drowned thousands of people, and makes men seasick when they sail on it? I am sure you would say that such a man was not guided by sound judgment. But I do not see how the case is any better with a man who complains of a very well-managed railroad because the principal owner of it is a very objectionable person.

VII.
THE RAILWAY QUESTION: ITS LITTLE SIDE.

I FANCY the reader complaining that in the preceding chapter I have ignored the strong objections which he urges against our railway management and considered only the weak ones. I admit that he is right to this extent: that I persisted in looking on the subject from a single standpoint, to wit, that of the interests of the great public, of whom we really see and hear very little, and considering whether, on the whole, that public was well served by the railways. I claim that this is the big side of the question.

But let us by all means hear the other side and weigh it impartially. So far as I know, its ablest and most authoritative representation is found in Mr. Hudson's book on "the Railways and the Republic," and in certain papers by Dr. R. T. Ely in Harper's Magazine, I commend these publications to the careful study of every man interested in the subject.

But I cannot pretend to answer their views and arguments, and that for two reasons. In the first place, if they could be answered it would take a big book to do it. In the next place, I am disposed to think that a good deal of what they say is true. They do, indeed, present only one side of the case, and I suspect that that side is a little exaggerated; but I do not object to this, because I am in favor of all measures which will improve our railway management, and, in order to secure such measures, the attention of the public must be loudly called to the subject.

But what I wish the reader to clearly understand is that this is the little side of the railway question and not its big side, and that the great facts which I set forth in my last talk are more important than all that can be said on the other side. Allow me to show by an illustration what I mean when I say that this is the big side of the question.

If a person should travel through the healthiest country in the world, search out all the sick, watch and describe their suffering, and then publish to the world what he had observed, he might make his readers believe it the most pestilential country on the globe. He could rival Milton in describing

"All maladies

Of ghastly spasm, or racking torture, qualms

Of heart-sick agony, all feverous kinds, Dropsies and asthmas and joint-racking rheums,"

in such terms that one would hardly dare to visit that country, and yet tell nothing but the truth.

But the person who wanted to know the real merits of the country would look into statistical tables in order to learn the death-rate per annum. If he found it to be only fifteen in a thousand he would know that the country was the healthiest in the world in spite of the melancholy picture. This little result of statistics would be a great big fact swallowing up all the little facts about the sufferers, because it would be a result founded on a consideration of all the cases of life and death in the whole population, while the facts set forth by the observer would only describe individual cases.

Just so with the railroad question. The fact that our great trunk lines of railway carry a ton of freight a thousand miles for six or seven dollars may seem like a little fact, but in reality it is a very big one, because it is a general average result of the price at which they serve all the millions of people who live in the Western and Middle States. Comparing it with the rates for similar services abroad, it shows that our railroads serve the public about as cheaply as any in the world, notwithstanding the drawbacks under which they labor arising from sparseness of population and high wages. This again shows that our railway management is among the best in the world, in the terms on which it serves the public. Every sensible man who is qualified to judge of the subject knows that on no other system could we get passengers or freight carried more cheaply than we now do. If the government of the United States should take possession of every railway in the country tomorrow there can hardly be a doubt that the average cost of freight transportation would be higher than it now is on the great trunk lines. This great big fact completely swallows up all the little facts that one or two railways have no fixed prices, and charge whatever they think a customer can be made to pay, that some others make discriminating rates, charging one man more than they do another for the same services, and that yet others charge more for a short haul than for along one. Carrying passengers forty miles an hour for two or three cents a mile is a fact which outweighs all we can say about watered stocks, just as the fact of the Etruria carrying a thousand passengers across the ocean at a speed of twenty miles an hour outweighs all we can say about the badness of the coffee these passengers have to drink.

Do not misunderstand me. I am not arguing against any measures which will improve our railway service. I go yet further and admit that this little side of the question is the one which requires most attention. If, in the healthy country we have just imagined, it was found that here and there people suffered from bad drainage, of course I would want the drainage improved. So with our railway service. What I think we ought to avoid is any policy which will discourage capitalists from building more railways. If we so hem these roads by restrictions that capitalists can no longer feel secure of a profit by running them, we shall simply stop their building until we adopt new measures, or give new guarantees to capitalists against loss.

I admit that there is much that is wrong in the relation of railroad corporations to the public. It is a wrong upon the people that nearly all our prominent and influential public men, including members of Congress and members of state legislatures, travel free wherever they wish to go. I am ready to do anything I can to correct this wrong. It is wrong that corporations of any kind can own and manage state legislatures. It is a wrong when courts are under the influence of such corporations. It is a wrong when a railroad charges one person more than another for the same service. We may consider these different wrongs from different points of view; for example, from one point of view with reference to their nature and remedy, and from another point with the object of understanding their connection with the benefits rendered by the roads. It is from the latter standpoint that the matter should first be considered.

The corrupting influence of railroad corporations upon state legislatures, and hence upon the public and upon politics in general, has been denounced in such terms as might imply that it would be better to have no roads than to suffer such demoralization as we are suffering and are likely to suffer from them. Even if this were true, which it is not, it is an exceedingly incomplete statement of the question, because it implies that the main fault is on the side of the railroads and corporations. It is not correct to say that corporations corrupt legislators. No influence can corrupt an honest man. If corporations practice bribery with success, it is only because they have corrupt men to deal with. Hence, to state the case exactly as it is, we ought to say that the corporations take advantage of the corruptibility of the men who form our state legislatures. They find them already corrupted, and act accordingly.

Now, if these legislators are corrupt, whose fault is it? Evidently it is the fault of the public who send bad men to represent them. It is, therefore, the voters who ought to be denounced for all this wickedness, and not the corporations. The real evil is that the average voter is nearly always ready to support his party's ticket, regardless of the character of the men whose names it bears. When the great mass of voters are determined that none but honest men shall represent them, and that none but honest methods shall be employed in politics, the evil will be cured, and it will not be cured before. Our first step is, then, to educate the people to a proper sense of their duties and rights.

If we now look at the matter from another point of view we shall see that the wholesale denunciation of corrupt practices which I have referred to tends to aggravate rather than cure the evil. The more respect the public has for the legitimate rights of a corporation, the less excuse that corporation has for trying to deceive the public. Vice versa, in a community where the rights of corporations are not duly respected, those bodies will necessarily seek to secure their rights by improper methods. The nearer public sentiment approaches to correct views in this respect, the more readily will great corporations let the public understand and see into their affairs.

Let us illustrate this by the watering of stocks. Suppose that some enterprise, it may be a copper-mine or it may be a railway, finds itself making very large profits. As a general rule it has a perfect right to all the profits it can make by legitimate business and lawful methods. But the stockholders know very well that if the public saw stock on which only thirty, forty, or fifty dollars a share had been paid going up to three hundred, five hundred, or a thousand dollars a share, there would be a loud complaint, and perhaps the state legislatures would be called upon to intervene and stop these exorbitant profits. So, in lieu of paying money dividends and leaving the shares to grow in value, the directors declare "stock dividends," which continually increase the number of shares held, so that the profits per share are kept down to a moderate percentage. The public at large is neither better nor worse off for this "watering," for the simple reason that the company will make as much money from the public as they can under any circumstances, and they cannot command any more after watering their stock than they could before.

"We may lay it down as a rule that nothing is more useless than the denunciation of individuals or bodies of men for acts which are in consonance with the general tendency of human nature. As a general rule such denunciation makes matters worse more than it helps them. "When a remedy is needed, it must be applied through public opinion, not by measures against the men complained of, but by changing the situation so that selfish men cannot take advantage of it. The cure for bribery of legislators is not reached by merely denouncing the men who bribe, but by sending honest men as representatives. Of course I do not mean to say that bribery should be condoned. I mean that there will be very little bribery where we have a sufficiently pure and elevated public opinion on the subject. Practically the courts and the laws represent public opinion. When the latter is controlled by a high moral standard there will be very little bribery, and that little will be speedily punished. When the moral standard is low, there will be plenty of bribery, do what we will, and we shall not be able to punish it in the courts. It is, therefore, to public education that we are to look for a cure.

Now let us get things in their true perspective. The facts which I have brought out in these talks are greater and more wide-reaching than any of the evils of railway management. Denounce the latter as we will, it remains true that the men who run railroads are the ablest business managers that the country has seen, that they serve the public cheaper than any other set of men could have done it, and that their work lies at the very basis of our civilization. To settle the question whether, as a class, they charge too much for their services, we must see what profits they make. It is said that during the past twelve months the railways of the country at large have not earned the current rate of interest upon the capital actually invested by their projectors. If this is true, it disposes at a single stroke of the complaint against high charges. As to their tyranny, all that can be said of it is disposed of by the great fact that not one person out of a hundred who reads these papers was ever consciously injured by a railroad corporation or ever received anything but benefits from it.

VIII.
HOW ONE MAN MAY DO
THE WORK OF TEN THOUSAND.

"There must be something wrong in a system under which one man can accumulate a hundred millions of dollars, and the people of this country are determined to do something towards rectifying it." We have all heard this sentiment in a thousand forms during the last few months. I am inclined to think that it voices the feeling on which the popular support of the labor movement is based. When the common man hears that somebody has gained one hundred millions of dollars, he naturally thinks that the system by which he gained it must have an element of injustice in it. If asked why any lack of justice, the common man would probably answer, that this rich man must have gained money which in equity belonged to other people. The question of equity is not, however, the only one to be considered. That of policy also comes into play. If it should turn out that the public at large were great gainers through some one person being allowed to accumulate a hundred million of dollars, we might dispense with the question of equity. But since equity as well as policy should come into consideration, I shall consider the subject from both points of view, beginning with the former.

In considering a question of equity we must agree upon some principle determining what we are to understand by that word. Now the customs of society have established the principle that if two men are rendering the same service, they should get the same price for it, no matter if it costs one ten times as much as it does the other. For example, if a very skilful dairyman should learn to make butter with half the work that other dairymen make it, and should bring that butter to a market where the selling price was forty cents a pound, it would not be equitable for the buyer to say to him: "Although I have been giving forty cents a pound for butter to others, yet I will only give you twenty cents, and will not allow any one else to give you more, because you make two pounds as easily as those other sellers make one." If the reader will not accept this principle, then he need not proceed any further in this chapter, because it is on this principle that the conclusions are based. But if he does accept it, then he must do so to its fullest extent, and admit that if one man does the work of ten thousand, there is nothing positively unjust in paying him the wages of ten thousand men. This may seem to be carrying the principle a great deal further, but still the principle itself remains the same. Questions of justice, considered apart from questions of policy, belong rather to the instincts than to the reason, and I confess that my instincts are such that I see nothing unjust in paying one man the wages of ten thousand for doing the work of ten thousand. Let us now see how a few men did the work of ten times as many thousand.

Before railways were built, the people of Boston, New York, Baltimore, and other cities could be supplied with flour only from farms near the seaboard or watercourses, or in the immediate neighborhood of the cities. A farmer in the middle of Pennsylvania, New York, or Ohio could not get his wheat to market without carting it to some canal or navigable river. So laborious was this to farmers who lived many miles from other means of transportation that they often burned their corn as fuel, because it did not pay to carry it to market. The reader may calculate for himself how many millions of men would be required to transport all the flour we eat from the farms to the cities on our Atlantic seaboard if we had no railways.

Fifty years ago the construction of railways was only fairly commenced; and it was doubtful if they could be successful on a large scale. But a few far-sighted capitalists saw that if such a road were built through New York State, a few thousand men, by running the railway, would do the work of as many millions in transporting the products of farms to the seaboard. Probably very few believed them. At least only a few men were ready to invest their fortunes in the enterprise, and so it was by these few that the new roads were first inaugurated on so large a scale. The result was that the productiveness of the inhabitants of New York State was increased many fold. The railroad was soon doing the work of a hundred thousand men; perhaps I should be nearer the truth if I said a million.

Now what ought the people of New York State to have said to the leading men of the enterprise when their roads got going? Should they have said: You are making too much money off of your road; although your organization is doing the work of a hundred thousand men, you are yourself only one man, and shall only have the pay of one man? It does not seem to me that this would have been right. But if we consider that it would be right to allow him the pay of more than one man for his services in building the road, by what principle shall we learn where to stop? If two men, why not three? If three, why not four? If four, why not a thousand? If a thousand, why not a hundred thousand?

Facts make the principle that govern the case. The projector might have said in reply: My railroad is doing the work of one hundred thousand men, and I must have the pay of one hundred thousand men as long as I live, and my heirs must have it as long as the road lasts. If we estimate the pay of one man to be five hundred dollars a year, he would then have been demanding fifty millions of dollars per year in perpetuity for his services.

But society did not concede any such claim on his part any more than it tried to restrict his profit to the pay of one man. It simply said to him, You have got your road and we will pay you the lowest price at which we can get our transportation done; but we give you notice that now, you having taught us what good a railway can do, we will build all the roads we want for ourselves, and we will not allow you a dollar more for what you do for us with your railroad than we have to pay other people for the same service. This, it seems to me, was the just and natural solution of the problem.

In the process we have been examining is involved a principle which it is most necessary to understand. We see it in all the operations of business and manufacture, yet we are prone to overlook it; I must, therefore, ask your careful attention to some further illustrations of it. Suppose a tribe of Patagonians who gain their subsistence by killing birds with bows and arrows. With the utmost industry, each of them can only kill, on an average, two birds a day. A lame but skilful civilized man comes among them with a supply of guns, sulphur, saltpetre, and lead. With the charcoal which they can supply him he proceeds to make gunpowder, and with the lead to mould bullets. He now says to them, It takes one of you a whole day to kill two birds. I cannot kill any birds at all myself because I am lame; but I can show you how each of you can kill, not two birds in a day, but fifty. Whoever makes powder and shot in the way I show, and uses one of my guns in the way I will direct, can kill forty-eight birds more per day than he now does. In return for this service you must give me half the extra birds which my skill enables you to shoot: that is, each of you must give me twenty-four birds out of every fifty, or their equivalent.

It is evidently for their interest to accept such an offer. He shows them how to get the charcoal by burning wood; he weighs out the materials for the powder, and shows them how to use them. He melts the lead and makes it into shot; shows them how to shoot, and very soon each man who uses one of the guns is bringing in fifty birds a day, which is more than they all can eat.

If the tribe is a hundred strong, its members are now, in combination with the owner of the guns, doing the work of twenty-five hundred men; and the owner is doing the work of twenty-four hundred men, and getting the pay of twelve hundred. Getting nearly half the whole product, he has nearly half as much to eat as the whole tribe.

Now, is there anything inequitable in this? If the tribe should say to him: "Look here, pale face; you have not shot a single bird, nor put in a stroke of work, unless you call it work to weigh out the materials for making powder. Our labor has made the powder; our legs have carried us through the swamps. You have no business getting more birds than any of the rest of us, and you shall have no more." Would that be exactly fair? Questions as to whether a thing is or is not fair must ultimately depend upon the inner conscience of the judge; so I leave this question to the conscience of the reader, only remarking that I myself see nothing wicked or unjust in the arrangement by which the one civilized man gets half the product.

Now what is the principle concealed in this illustration? It is that labor alone is not sufficient to produce the things necessary for our welfare to the best advantage. To make a pair of boots to the best advantage requires something more than the mere labor put into them. It requires the know-how and the show-how. Just as the Patagonians gained their birds through the help of the man who did no shooting, but knew how it ought to be done, and showed them how to do it; so boots are made, not merely by tanners and bootmakers alone, but by the labor of these men combined with the knowledge and direction of business-managers. Clearly the latter are entitled to a share in the product.

You reply, perhaps, Grant that they are entitled to a share. But a great many of them get too large a share.

But by what principle will you decide what share they shall get? Must they all get the same share? In that case the good manager and the bad manager would be paid exactly the same profits. The latter might buy poor leather, might fail to take good care of it, might let his machinery be badly used, might mismanage his business in every way without suffering for it, if you adopted any such principle. It is evident that we must have some way of letting a good manager get more of the product than a bad one. If you reflect how difficult it would be to find out whether the business was well or badly managed, you will see the impossibility of fixing any definite rate of profit for the manager.

This correct rate of profit, which it would be so hard for the wisest man to fix by investigation, is determined by our system of free competition among managers. We simply say to every manager: "Do the very best you can. Direct your men in the most efficient way you know how, and manage your business with the least waste. Whatever profits you can make in this way over and above your fellow-managers you are entitled to, and no more. If they do better, then you must go into some other business. If you do better than any of them, take the profit which will thus come to you."

Please remember that under our system no man and no body of men is required to work under a manager, and to accept his know-how and show-how, if he does not want to do so. Every workman in the factory, every bricklayer who helps in building a house, is at perfect liberty to sell his own services directly to the public if he finds it advantageous so to do. If workmen find that the managers who direct them are getting an undue share of the proceeds, they are at perfect liberty to form co-operative associations, and thus secure all the profits themselves. But, if they find that they get better wages from the manager than they can earn by working for themselves, then there is nothing inequitable in the manager getting as much advantage of his skill as the competition of his fellow-managers will permit his getting.

In view of these facts it seems to me that the quotation with which I opened this talk should be expressed thus:

"There must be something wrong in a system under which one man is allowed to render a hundred million dollars' worth of services to his fellow-men, and the people of this country are determined to do something towards rectifying it."

IX.
WAS IT GOOD FOR US THAT WE ALLOWED ONE MAN TO MAKE A HUNDRED MILLION DOLLARS?

The reader may possibly object to the last chapter, that it dealt in the equities of the case, and therefore had a little too much sentiment mixed up with it. He may say that it is not a question of equity at all, but one of public advantage or disadvantage, and may claim that the subject should be treated from this point of view.

I am perfectly willing to discuss the subject on this basis, because then the foundation is a great deal stronger than before. If you choose to follow me carefully, leisurely, and thoughtfully, you cannot fail to see that it is for your good and for mine that any man who wants to be a capitalist, and who has a talent for business management, should be allowed to gain all the wealth he can, whether one million dollars or one hundred millions, by legitimate business enterprises; and that the more he gains in this way the better for us all.

The common belief seems to be that, when a man gets very rich, he does it by collecting wealth which, but for him, would have been gained by somebody else, who, perhaps, deserved it better. There are few or no opinions, generally held by men, which are false under all conditions and in their entirety. So, before we deny this popular doctrine, let us see in what cases it may be true. There is, undoubtedly, a great deal of speculation in the business world in which one man can gain only what another loses. It amounts to about the same thing as betting on the future prices of stocks or goods. Thousands of people go into Wall Street to speculate. The large majority are the so-called "lambs," who are not so wise as they think. The sharper men win the bets made with them, and thus grow rich.

Fortunes won in this way are not of the slightest concern to any one except those who make or lose. None of your interests are affected by some Wall Street shark gaining a hundred dollars or a thousand from each of a thousand other speculators. If you do not want to suffer, all you have to do is to keep out of Wall Street. If you have been a "lamb" you have only yourself to blame. If you have not, you have lost nothing. Leaving out this exceptional case, which, as I have said, is of no public concern to anybody but those who engage in speculation, the only way in which a man can make a fortune of one hundred million dollars is by doing one hundred million dollars' worth of good, probably several times over, to his fellow-men.

The question now before us may be considered under several different aspects. We might first inquire whether there is any possible way of stopping a man who wants to be rich from making all the money he can. If we found that this was not possible, we might dispose of the whole matter by saying that it is of no use to trouble ourselves about it because we cannot help ourselves. But I do not propose to dispose of the question in this simple way. I want the reader to put the question to himself in such forms as the following:

If we could persuade or force a man not to accumulate more than a certain fixed amount of wealth—say one hundred thousand dollars—would it be to our interest to do so?

If, when Mr. Cornelius Vanderbilt had made one hundred thousand dollars, he had said to himself, "This is as much wealth as one needs or ought to possess; I will, therefore, retire from business, and make no more money," would we have been better or worse off on account of that resolution on his part? To answer this question, we must examine the history of the case, and learn how Cornelius Vanderbilt gained his wealth. The reader probably knows this as well as I do; so all I need to do is to give a short summary of the well-known facts in the case.

When still quite young, Cornelius Vanderbilt was the owner of several small steamboats, which he managed himself. He was so successful that, before reaching middle age, he was, for those times, a very wealthy man. Did he become so by injuring any one else? I think not. He never forced a man on board his boat who did not want to go; never carried a pound of freight which the owner did not want carried; never charged more for fare or freight than the people to whom he rendered the service were willing to give. Nobody ever paid him for his service more than he would have had to pay any one else. His only advantage lay in the fact that he knew how to render more service at a given outlay of labor and money than anybody else did. He bought the kind of boats which other people found it pleasant to travel upon. He sent them to the places where they were most wanted, and took people where they most wanted to go, at the times most convenient for them. He selected good men to run his boats, and, while putting into them whatever the public liked to have, he was careful never to waste labor or money in doing what people did not want done.

As he made money he bought more steamboats, thus extending his operations over a much wider area than before. Thus he carried more and more people where they wanted to go, and brought more and more goods where they were wanted. It was through becoming rich that he was enabled to build these new boats; and, having built them, he managed them on the same principle as before; that is, he sent them where thousands of people were most desirous to go, and brought goods from various parts of the continent to the places where people most wanted them.

When he had thus gained several millions of dollars by rendering, we may suppose, a dollar's worth of service to each of several millions of people, he saw that railway managers did not work together to the best advantage, and did not convey their millions of passengers and their enormous quantities of freight in the most advantageous and economical manner. So he proceeded to purchase the stock of the Harlem Railroad, the Hudson River, the New York Central, and the Lake Shore and Michigan Southern, and finally succeeded in inducing the owners of a line of road extending all the way from New York to Chicago to place the whole under his management. The result of this was, that he brought the breadstuffs of the West to New York State more cheaply and expeditiously than they were ever brought before, and thus enabled millions of people to buy their flour at a lower price than they would otherwise have had to pay.

As in his early steamboat life he never demanded from one of his million of passengers more money for a ticket than the passenger deemed it to his advantage to pay, and never charged a dollar more freight than merchants were willing to give. Competing lines were in operation, and every one had the right to send by other lines, or not to send at all. The result was a continual addition to his fortune, amounting to several millions of dollars a year.

At this point, dear reader, do not abandon business for sentiment by saying that I am eulogizing a very selfish man. I am only stating the essential facts and leaving out the non-essential ones. You may, if you choose, call him a greedy, grasping, bloated, inhuman being. But that would be mere sentiment and not business. If the ten millions of people to whom he brought bread all the way from Chicago, and the hundreds of millions whom he carried on his railway were benefited by the services, as they undoubtedly were, his personal qualities do not affect the question at all. Not one man out of a thousand ever set eyes upon him, or was in any way injured by his selfishness. Let us, therefore, confine ourselves to a business view of the facts.

Suppose, now, that Mr. Vanderbilt, when he found his little steamboats so successful that he had gained a hundred thousand dollars from them, had said: "This is money enough for one man, and I will now let some one else manage this business, while I, to show my belief in the dignity and rights of labor, will work as a mere hand on a steamboat." What would have been the result? The enterprise which subsequently sent a line of steamers to Galveston and the Isthmus would either have been wanting, or would have been delayed for several years. A million of people would have had to wait two or three years for the advantages of shipping and travelling which Vanderbilt gave them ; and, when they finally got them, the boats would not have been so much to their liking, and freights would have been higher. We may suppose that the disadvantage of a million of people would have averaged one or two dollars a year to each person for a number of years. Of course they would never have been aware of these disadvantages, nor think that the eccentric man who was working as a common hand when he had the ability to be a first-class manager would have served them much better had he continued to manage. But their ignorance would not have changed the fact that here would have been a great waste of valuable power.

So with the railways. If Vanderbilt had not got control of the roads I have described, the unity of management which is so necessary in working a road would have been delayed for several years—perhaps until the present time—so that freight and passengers would not have been carried so expeditiously as they now are. Moreover, the managers, not being so able as Vanderbilt to prevent all loss and waste on the road, people would probably have had to pay a little more on the average for their tickets. Thus everybody would have been worse off, rather than better. It is on a large scale what we supposed to take place among the Patagonians in our last talk. The man who merely showed them how to use a gun benefited not only himself, but them also, by enabling them to get food much more advantageously than before.

But there is more yet to be said. Before we can consider the question satisfactorily settled we must inquire who got the benefit of Vanderbilt's money? Did he or the public get the good of it? Here I have to make a statement which at first blush may appear a paradox; but it appears so only to those who have failed to look clearly at the facts. I say that Vanderbilt never got any use of his money, except his board, clothing, house-rent, and appliances for the personal pleasure and comfort of himself and friends. The sole benefit of all the rest of his wealth went entirely to the public. It is one of the great vices of our times that we think and talk about wealthy men as if they had the sole enjoyment of their wealth. But all they really enjoy is the laborious privilege of managing it and the sentimental pleasure of calling it theirs. If Vanderbilt had said, "Now this is my railroad, and I shall not carry freight on it for anybody else, and will only bring food for my own family and give excursions to my own friends," then the case would have been different and the road would have been of no use to the public. But of all the freight brought over the road, how much did Mr. Vanderbilt ever get? Of course, you know very well, not enough to even think of or mention.

But, you may reply, everybody else who got freight carried over his road had to pay him for it. Very well, what did he do with the money they paid him? Nine tenths of it he paid to laborers. With a good part of the other tenth he laid new steel rails over the whole road from New York to Chicago, by which passengers and freight were brought more quickly and cheaply than ever before. For whose benefit was that? Evidently it was for the benefit of the passengers and the public, because after the steel rails were laid they paid Vanderbilt less money for the service than they did before, and they got carried faster. But, you may say, they still had to pay him. Yes, but how insignificant the amount they paid him compared with the value of the service rendered. Let us again ask what he did with the money he received for this important service? A portion of it he expended in building himself a house and filling it with pictures and furniture. What he expended in this way was all that he applied to his own uses. It was a small fraction of what he received for freight. He spent the remainder directly or indirectly in building new roads and in other business enterprises for the public. When I say he did this indirectly I mean that he loaned the money to others to expend in this way, and thus enabled them to build railroads and steamboats, which they otherwise could not have built.

I think I have made it clear beyond a cavil that it was to your benefit and my benefit that Vanderbilt did not stop making money, to become a steamboat hand, but that his grasping love of wealth prompted him to engage in managing steamboats and railways with such success that he accumulated more than a hundred millions of dollars. I hope Vanderbilts will continue to arise until our whole industrial organization is so perfected that everything we want shall be made and brought to us at the lowest possible price.

ON THE LABOR QUESTION.

X.
THE CAPITALIST AND WHAT
HE HAS DONE FOR US.

The lessons I have tried to teach in the last two chapters are so important that I must beg leave to recapitulate and enforce some of their points. I deem this necessary for the very reason that they are conclusions which run counter to our ordinary notions.

One of the notions to which I allude is, that wealth is accumulated for the sole benefit of its owner: for instance, that Vanderbilt's hundred millions went for Vanderbilt's sole benefit, so that nobody else has any interest in it, or at least only a slight interest. Yet it is only necessary to open our eyes and look closely at the state of the case to see that this notion is all wrong. The great proposition, to which all that I have said converges, is that great accumulations of capital, whether by an individual or a corporation, are really employed for the public benefit, so that all get the good of them.

What did Vanderbilt's wealth originally consist in? As I showed in the last chapter, one of its large items were the steel rails which were laid from New York to Chicago. If he and his associates had not accumulated great fortunes they could never have commanded the money to purchase these rails, and the bread which you and I now eat could not have been brought so cheaply from the West to our homes. In a word, Vanderbilt's great wealth consisted very largely in railroads employed, not for his benefit, but for that of the public, and from which he did not get materially more good than anybody else did, because even the dividends which he gained were expended in enlarging and improving the roads.

Now what is true of this particular part of Vanderbilt's fortune is true of all the accumulations of the capitalists, great and small. A capitalist may be defined as a man who saves up his money to gain interest upon it. But the only way in which he can gain interest is by employing it for the benefit of his fellow-men, or getting somebody else to employ it in this way. That is to say, the money which he saves goes to build a railway for conveying goods to and from distant communities, a factory to make clothes for the continually increasing population, a ship to convey goods to a foreign country, a house to be occupied by people who cannot afford to buy one for themselves, or some other permanent agency for supplying the public wants.

This point is so important that I must ask leave to illustrate it by continuing our little romance about the visitor to the Patagonians. We left him with a food supply of twenty-four hundred birds a day, contributed to his support by the tribe. This would be too absurd to continue, because the whole tribe could not eat half of what was shot. The tribe would say: "We cannot possibly eat all these birds, let us stop and build better wigwams." So the lame man would say," instead of shooting all those birds for me, go to work and build me a hundred wigwams. You must make one of them very fine for my occupation, but the others are to be my property to dispose of as I please." When this is done the question arises, What will the man do with all those wigwams? As he can only occupy one of them, he can only say to the tribe, "Occupy the others yourselves, and pay me what rent you can for them." But when he got the rent he could do nothing with it but get other things for the support of himself and the tribe, and so in the end the latter would be getting nearly all the benefit of the man's skill, and this by the sheer necessity of the case. I think none of their moralists and philosophers would lament a state of things in which one man should be allowed to own a hundred wigwams.

The fact is that until we think carefully over the subject we can have no conception how valuable one man's foresight and enterprise may be to millions of his fellow-citizens. I recollect, in speaking to an intelligent and thoughtful Knight of Labor of the value of Vanderbilt's enterprise, he raised what was, in principle, the very sound objection that if Vanderbilt had not done what he did somebody else would, and that there was therefore no particular reason why Vanderbilt should reap so large a reward. I say the principle on which this objection was founded is perfectly correct, because if there are three, ten, or fifty people capable, without any extraordinary sacrifice on their own part, of rendering services worth many millions of dollars to their fellows, it is perfectly just that they should be made to compete with each other until their compensation is brought down to its lowest point. If then there were twenty or fifty men able and ready to do what Vanderbilt did, it would have been perfectly right that society should have commanded their services on the cheapest terms it could.

But let us now look closely at the matter and see how what may seem to us at first sight a most insignificant fact may have very important consequences. The reason why Vanderbilt was able to collect so large a sum from the public for services rendered was not merely that nobody else could have rendered these services at any time, but that he was the only man in the field at the moment ready and willing to go ahead with his enterprises. Now let us calculate the money value to the public of this mere willingness to go ahead, coupled with the ability to see further than his fellow-men did. At a moderate calculation there were, fifty or sixty years ago, ten millions of people to whom a railway system connecting New York with what was then the West would have been worth ten cents a day each, or say thirty dollars a year. This being the case, if Vanderbilt's enterprise did nothing more than get each section of the road and each step in its management into operation a year sooner than others would have done, he rendered his fellows a service worth three hundred millions of dollars, merely by his foresight and courage, to say nothing of his organizing ability.

Successful capitalists are for the most part the sharpest business men of the community. This goes almost without saying, for otherwise they would never have amassed wealth, or, if they had amassed it, would have lost it when they went into business. What do we mean when we say that some prominent man is a sharp man of business? Judging from the newspapers and the addresses at labor assemblies, we should suppose this to mean that the man had learned the art of cheating other people out of the results of their labor. I have shown in previous talks how groundless this notion is, and so instead of discussing it further shall try to find the true answer to the question. A sharp man of business on a large scale—I mean one who successfully manages new and great enterprises—is one who is quick to see what large bodies of people want, and expert in the rare art of building up organized systems to supply that want. We are so accustomed to organized systems thus built up that we seldom think how much more they involve than the men and appliances concerned with them.

Take a railway for example. Of material things it includes a road-bed, the rails, the station, the engines, and the cars. Of men it includes engineers, brakemen, conductors, and other employees to the number of thousands. But much more than all this was necessary in order that the railroad might perform its functions. Before a single tie was laid, before a man was engaged to dig out the road-bed, it was necessary to decide where the road should start from, through what towns it should pass, and whither it should end. Here the business qualities of the capitalist come in. The man who decides these things successfully is one who knows what thousands of his fellow-men want, not only now, but for the future; where towns are likely to grow up, and what products will be wanted at the terminus of the road. The labor of thousands of men is to be employed for one or more years in laying the road, making the rails, and building the engines and stations. It depends upon the talent and sound judgment of the originators whether this labor shall be in great part wasted by being of little service to anybody, or whether it shall supply a hundred thousand people with just the means of transportation that they most want. Now, if every man was born with the talent necessary for deciding where the road should run, for knowing where to find the best engineers to lay the road out, and to calculate the excavations necessary; how and where to get the engines built, and how to find the men to run them, and then how to organize their work, the case would be entirely different from what it is. As a matter of fact only one man out of ten thousand can do all this successfully, and only one out of a hundred thousand can do it in the most effective way. If we could value men by the services they render we might say of the best organizer in the United States: Here is a man who can so organize railroads through populous districts as to save a million of his fellow-men a dollar a year each by securing them cheaper transportation than they can otherwise get. He is therefore worth to them a million dollars a year.

Then, after the road is built and in operation, it may be worth a million dollars a year to its owners and to the men who use it to have it managed in the very best way. You may have the road completed, with the engines and cars and men all at work, and yet the result may be a failure. Men are continually leaving or changing their occupations, and new ones must be got to fill their places. Some one must decide what duties every man shall perform and must see that he is trained in their performance. There must be a system by which every one of the thousands of employees shall do the right thing, in the right place, and at the right time; if he does not, accidents will happen, passengers will be killed, and freight will be lost or delayed. Now this is something which does not happen of itself, but requires a body of managers of rare qualities, to do everything in the best way.

I hope I have justified my definition that the sharp and successful man of business is simply one who can render great services to all the people who make up the state. What have such men done? The question will answer itself if we will only look around us.

They have promoted everything that is good in this nineteenth century. They have not only built railways from the Atlantic to the Pacific Ocean, and set them going, but they have founded schools and colleges and built churches. Had no one ever got rich we should have had no colleges except a few miserable ones supported by the state; we should have had no railways; flour would have been worth ten dollars a barrel and upward in all cities; labor organizations would have been unknown, because no laborer could ever have spared the time to organize or have saved the money necessary to make his influence felt.

XL.
WHAT CAPITAL HAS DONE FOR THE LABORER.

We have all heard a great deal of talk about the great conflict between labor and capital. We have discussed this conflict so ardently as to forget all about the actual facts of the case; and, indeed, I doubt if one man out of twenty who engages in the discussion ever stops to think what capital really is. If one would only stop to study out the question he would see that no such conflict could have any sound reason for going on, and, in fact, could hardly arise among sensible men. In saying this I do not deny that there is always a kind of contest in progress. Laborers want, and rightfully want, the highest wages they are able to command. Employers want, and rightfully want, to induce them to work as cheaply as possible. But the efforts to which the two parties are thus led do not differ, in their original nature, from those which have been going on ever since men began to make progress, and which must continue as long as humanity exists under its present conditions. Everybody who sells goods wants to get as much as he can for them, and everybody who buys wants to get them as cheaply as he can. Sellers are on the search for good buyers, and buyers are on the lookout for good bargains. In the same way, laborers are on the lookout for good employers, and employers are seeking for cheap and efficient laborers. To call a contest thus arising a conflict between labor and capital is as great a misnomer as it would be to call a higgling and dispute between a man and his butcher a conflict between money and beef. It is not the beef the man is quarreling with, but it is the owner of the beef. It is not the money the butcher is dealing with, but the man. In the same way the laborer is dealing, not with capital, but with the owner of capital. This misuse of words is, really, a source of great drawback to clear thinking, because it leads people to mistake the interests of society, and to engage in efforts which can do nothing but harm to all. To avoid this evil, let us see how capital and capitalists arose.

In our colonial times there was very little that we should now call capital; only such things as the horses, ploughs, and farm-buildings, the implements of the farmer, the stock in trade of the shop-keeper, and the tools of the mechanic. How does it happen that we have any more capital now than in colonial times? We can readily imagine everything to have gone on, up to the present time, just as it did in those times, without railways, steam machinery, great warehouses, paved streets, fine furniture. Why did things not continue so? I reply, it was because certain people were not satisfied with what they had, but wanted to get rich, and knew how to do it. Now, when a man wanted to get rich, how did he have to go to work? Robbery and gambling aside, there was but one possible way; he must do something that his fellow-men wanted to have done, and which they wanted so badly that they were willing to pay a great deal of money to get it done. No man could earn a dollar except by doing something for his fellow-men which they were willing to pay a dollar to have done, and hence something which they valued at more than one dollar.

Such, I say, was the problem presented to every man who wanted to make money. Now, if a man was only a common laborer, and could do nothing more for his fellow-men than hundreds or thousands of fellow-laborers could do, he could not possibly get rich very fast, although he might make a comfortable living. Hence, in order to attain his end, the man who wanted to get rich must make, buy, or borrow some kind of appliances, implements, or machinery which would enable him to do more work for his fellow-men than he could do without the appliances. For example, some of these men found that, by establishing a line of stages between two towns, they could render valuable services to hundreds or thousands of their fellow-men who wanted to travel, or to send goods from one city to another. So they bought horses and stage-coaches, built houses of entertainment, and set to work carrying passengers, materials, and goods. The horses, coaches, stables, and houses of entertainment were then the capital of these men. By the aid of that capital they rendered their fellow-men services many times greater than they could have rendered without the capital. If they planned their work with judgment and skill, so as to take people just when and where they wanted to be taken in the greatest numbers, they made money, and thus many of them got rich.

Now notice certain necessary conditions of these enterprises. It was impossible to get the money to buy the horses and coaches and build the stables unless some one saved up money which he could have spent had he chosen to do so. A man who spent all his income in food and clothing could never have got money to buy a coach. True, he might have borrowed the money from his neighbor. But then the neighbor must have saved the money up, and not spent it on food and clothing, else he never would have had any to loan. Possibly the owner of the coach might have bought it on credit; but, in this case, the maker of the coach must have been able to save the money necessary to buy the material and pay the wages of his workmen. We thus reach two great conclusions:

Firstly, without capital we should all now be in as poor a condition as our forefathers were in colonial times.

Secondly, we would never have had the capital unless men had wanted to get rich, and had saved up money to expend in making or buying things with which to render greater services to their fellow-men than they could render without them.

If, from these small beginnings of capital, we come down to the present time, we shall see that exactly the same principles are now at play as were at play when the first line of stages was set a going. Our great railway managers were the successors of the early stage-drivers; but, instead of dealing with a few hundreds of men, they are dealing with millions. They could never have built their railway unless the stockholders had saved up money to invest in the shares or bonds, which money was necessary to pay the wages of the men who built the road. Another important point is, that they did this of their own free will, and not because any law compelled them. No law could ever have been passed compelling Mr. Vanderbilt to build and run steamboats, or requiring the builders of the great railways to invest their capital in such enterprises.

What, then, is capital? I answer, capital means the houses we are living in, the farms and farming implements which produce our food, the cattle on the plains from which we get beef, the warehouses which hold our great stocks of food and clothing, the machinery which makes us clothing to wear, and the railways which bring things where we can get them. Talking about the oppressiveness of capital is the same thing as talking about the oppressiveness of food, clothing, machinery, and locomotives; that is, it is pure nonsense. All that capital can possibly do for us is to supply our wants. It can no more be used to oppress the masses than a wagon-load of bread can be used to starve them. It is impossible for the capitalist himself to get any benefit from his capital unless he uses it to benefit his fellow-men.

I now fancy the reader to ask, Do you then claim that we are in no danger at all from the powers of great corporations, whose operations extend over the whole country? Can the whole population of a city or a state afford to depend upon a few powerful and compact organizations for its supply of the necessaries of life? If the consolidation of capital goes on for fifty years as it has for the past twenty it is possible that a few great establishments will do nearly all the manufacturing for the land. Can we afford to leave them entirely unrestricted? To all this I reply:

Firstly, granting that we are going to subject these corporations to legislative control, the very first prerequisite of such action is a clear perception of the functions of the capitalist and of his relation to the rest of the community, as I have tried to set them forth. Hence, if you choose, you may consider me a believer in some such control, and you may consider that I have uttered these talks in order to promote intelligent control. At the same time I freely admit that I am not wise enough to plan any system of state regulation of industry, nor to foresee what form such a system will take if it is wisely adopted. To repeat once more what I have already said, I am no theorist, have worked out no system, and make no pretension to doing anything more than apply the common-sense of a common man to the study of the subject.

Secondly, as things just now look, it seems to me that the interests of the public, and therefore of laborers, who make up the greater part of the public, are in greater danger from labor organizations than they are from capitalists. Whatever may be the faults of the latter, their influence is essentially conservative. It will always be directed towards keeping the mills, machinery, and railroads on which we all depend in good working order. That these appliances should be kept in good working order is as important to us as that a ship in which we are crossing the ocean should be kept properly trimmed.

Thirdly, I think that whatever restrictions may be placed upon great corporations will come by judicial decisions, following each other so slowly, and each looking so small in itself, that the public will hardly notice them. I doubt whether we shall get much effective legislation either from Congress or the states; but on this point I am not at all dogmatic. I am willing to let the future keep its secrets.

PART III.
THE LABORER AND HIS WAGES

XII.
VISION OF A PURITAN DEACON.

How interesting and instructive it would be if we could get some Witch of Endor to raise from the dead the spirit of one of our ancestors, that we might show him our modern life and see what view he would take of it. I am sure if the reader could bring before him a New England deacon of a hundred and fifty years ago, to show him our houses, and hear his comments, he would feel himself a wiser man. Unfortunately, witches of all kinds disappeared from the face of the earth more than a century ago, so that we cannot call them to our aid. But I find there is another method of getting at the deacon's thoughts, which we shall have no difficulty in putting into operation. All who have read "Paradise Lost," know that the Archangel Michael once paid a visit to Adam in Paradise. By purging Adam's eyes with certain rare plants, which have remained in existence to this day, the archangel was enabled to show him events many centuries in advance of their occurrence. In accordance with this ancient precedent, I propose to bring Michael down to the house of Deacon Samuel Cushing, a well-to-do farmer, a God-fearing citizen, and a pillar of the Church, who resided in Cambridge, New England, in the year 1727. The object of the visit is to show the deacon the interior of a skilled laborer's dwelling, as we find it in this generation, and to listen to his remarks as the wonders of modern life are unfolded to him. So he is taken up into the world of visions, carried a century and a half into the future, and wafted into a little house, such as we now see in all our cities.

The vision of the cosey little parlor strikes him with wonder. The paper on the walls, exceeding in richness of coloring everything he had before seen; the pictures, the softly cushioned chairs, the finely painted woods, the family photographs on the mantel, the clock ticking in their midst, the gaudy chandeliers, the melodeon in the corner, with its polished case and ivory keys, are all objects of splendor, such as he had never before seen. The extravagance of the window curtains, which seem to him of the finest and costliest lace, might well call down his condemnation. Looking into the next room, he sees a lady dressed like the governor's wife, wearing an apron of the finest muslin, making tea with an apparatus wholly new to his eye. The snow-white sugar, the China cups, the costly table-cloth, the wonderful white bread, all excite his curiosity. Yet more incredible are the objects in the bedroom. Such a pile of pure white linen apparel, such gaudy bed-quilts, such finely made shirts, are quite new to his eye. But before he gets through his examination a sound is heard in the direction of the parlor. He returns to it and sees two beings enter, whom he, at the first glance, takes for fairies. They are two little children dressed in a profusion of needle-worked muslin garments of so singular a shape that he cannot tell whether they are girls or boys. His first impulse is to condemn such extravagance. "Is it possible," he says, "that the rich men of our posterity will be allowed to make such a display of their extravagance?"

Michael (who has forgotten how to talk poetry, and knows only plain English prose): "Who do you think lives in these rooms?"

Deacon. "I suppose some governor; or, more likely yet, it is some wealthy nobleman, who will come over here from England to corrupt our people by his ostentation and extravagance."

Michael. "Not at all, my good fellow. The man who lives in this house is a bricklayer."

Deacon. "A bricklayer!"

Michael. "Yes; he is just coming in. See him."

Surely enough, a bricklayer appears, carrying his kit and dinner-pail, and walks into the parlor with the air of a man who owns it. He goes up to the bedroom, washes the mortar off his plebeian hands in a splendid earthen basin, puts on one of the fine linen shirts, and soon goes down again, dressed as finely as the governor. He takes his seat at the table and commences his meal. The lady pours out his tea, into which he puts a profusion of the priceless white sugar.

Deacon. "A bricklayer at home in such a little palace, sitting on such finely cushioned chairs, and eating such food off such a table. How can it be? And what quantities of butter ho is putting on his bread! A bricklayer eating butter with white bread, wearing shoes all summer, and putting on fine shirts! How can it be? Do tell me what a bricklayer is doing in such a house, and who is that fine lady waiting on him?"

Michael. "That fine lady is his wife, attending to her every-day duties."

Deacon. "Where are her spinning-wheel and loom?"

Michael. "They have neither spinning-wheel nor loom in the house."

Deacon. "And those extravagant little beings; I thought they were fairies?"

Michael. "They are his children, two little girls who have just come in from hearing music in the public park."

Deacon. "But how can a bricklayer ever have such wealth, such a house, such a wife, and such children?"

Michael. "There is nothing uncommon about it. All men sober and industrious enough to learn a trade will be able to have such a house, such a wife, and such children in these coming days."

Deacon. "But how can all this be brought about? Why there is a year's work in the curtains to that man's window, and another year's work, I should think, in making these dresses of his wife and children, to say nothing of all the pictures, ornaments, and furniture in his house; and yet you say they have no spinning-wheel and no loom. How did they make such clothes?"

Michael. "It would be a long story to tell you in detail; but I will try to give you some idea of the process. All the cunningly wrought things you have seen are hardly made by hands at all, but by ingenious machines, one of which will turn out in an hour more work than a man can do in a year. These machines will be worked by engines more powerful than a thousand horses. They will turn out such quantities of goods that their owners will hardly know what to do with them. Then great leaders will rise and show men how, by working together in thousands, they can build roads and lay rails from one end of the state to the other, and from one end of the continent to the other. Then they will invent engines which will carry a hundred wagon-loads of the goods you have seen across whole colonies with the speed of a race-horse. Thus with the machine making the goods and the engines transporting them to every part of the country, everybody will be able to buy them. As an example of this, look at the bricklayer once more and see what be is doing."

Deacon. "He is eating grapes; but such luscious grapes I never dreamed of. Where did they come from?"

.Michael. "They came from the coast of the Pacific Ocean. One of these railroads will extend all the way across the continent and bring fresh grapes from the Pacific Ocean to this bricklayer's home in Massachusetts."

Deacon. "How the people will bless these machines, as they get to work. Even if they will be, as you say, inanimate objects, I do not .see how they can help crowning them with garlands of flowers."

Michael. "Nothing of the sort. The introduction of the machines will be cursed at every step, and great numbers of them will be destroyed by the indignant multitude."

Deacon. "That is the most incomprehensible thing you have yet said. How can it be?"

.Michael. "When the machines go into operation they make goods so cheaply that human hands cannot compete- with them, and thus laborers will find their work taken away from them. Thus the nail-makers will oppose the introduction of machinery for making nails, the cloth-maker will oppose the introduction of machinery for making cloth, and so on through the whole range of trades and occupations."

Deacon. "Then how will the machines ever get introduced at all?"

Michael. "Through the persistence and selfishness of the men who make and own them. They will force their machines into use in spite of all opposition, and make money by underselling everybody who has not got the machinery, and thus the machine itself will triumph in the long run."

Deacon. "But these great leaders of men, who show them how to make a railroad from one end of the continent to the other; they, if not the machines, will be crowned with garlands of flowers and received like heroes wherever they go."

Michael. "There again you are mistaken; they will be looked upon as the most selfish of mortals, and people will taunt them with their inability to take their railroads with them when they die."

Deacon. "Is all gratitude, then, to disappear from the breast of man within one hundred and fifty years? What possible object could these men have had in showing how the railway was to be built, if they got nothing but hard words in return?"

Michael. "Their motives will be purely selfish, as men suppose selfishness to be. They get their roads built in order that they may have the pleasure of owning them, and thus of being very rich men."

Deacon. "But how will that give them pleasure?"

Michael. "I cannot explain it, except by saying that such will be the propensity of human nature. Men will go to great labor in building roads, canals, and machinery of no more use to themselves than to their millions of fellow-citizens just from the innate impulse of their nature. That is all I can tell you about it."

Deacon. "What happy beings they will all be. I fear they will no longer believe in the fall of man nor in total depravity, and will indeed be so well satisfied with this world as never to want another."

Michael. "On the contrary, the year 1887, which I am now showing you, will be an era of such dissatisfaction with their lot on the part of skilled laborers as the world never before saw."

Deacon. "Dissatisfaction! At first sight I should hardly believe it possible. But I suppose it must always be true that wealth alone cannot make a man perfectly satisfied. After he has got all his wants supplied and is rolling in luxury he still finds that he needs something which wealth cannot give. Please tell me, then, what the laborers will want besides wealth."

Michael. "Dear Deacon, they will be dissatisfied because they think they do not get their fair share of riches. Orators and public speakers will tell them that the whole effect of railroads and machinery has been to make the rich richer and the poor poorer; and that laborers have a harder time to get along than they ever had before."

Deacon. "Then will all intelligence, all knowledge of the past, disappear from among men in that nineteenth century?"

Michael. "Not in their own opinion. They will boast that intelligence, virtue, and truth never reigned as they will then."

Deacon. "But you surely do not mean to say that any one can persuade that bricklayer, who has just finished such a supper as no governor of Massachusetts ever ate, that he is a suffering and abused man."

Michael. "I do say that very thing. Moreover, there is a side of the case which we have not yet seen. Neither the fine clothes of his wife and children, nor the delicious food which he eats, nor the ornaments which decorate his house, take all his wages to buy. He still has some surplus income which he puts into the fund of a great organization of men like himself, extending over the whole country, and called Knights of Labor."

Deacon. "I hope the money is wisely expended. But what you have said about the machines and other matters makes me fearful on the subject."

Michael. "I will let you judge for yourself. You see that great news-letter which the man has before him; can you see what he is reading?"

Deacon. "No; nothing but the heading. I see in big letters the words 'The Great Boycott,' but I do not know what that means."

Michael. "I will tell you. You have seen the luscious grapes which the man was eating, and which I told you came from the Pacific coast. "Well, the way he happened to have those grapes was that a great number of Chinese sailed all the way over the Pacific Ocean to California, and went to work for very low wages in various occupations, among them that of raising grapes, some of which were brought over to Massachusetts by the railway, Now these Knights of Labor, to which this bricklayer belongs, get very angry with these Chinese because they cultivate the grapes so cheaply; and last week they all put their heads together and decreed that no products of Chinese labor should come from California to Massachusetts. So the order was issued last week that not a man should run a train with California grapes on it; and the latter are rotting on the road between Massachusetts and California. While they are rotting the men who would have been transporting them are out of employment, and this man is paying money to support them while they stand idle and let the grapes rot."

Deacon. "You are reversing human nature in a way that is perfectly incomprehensible. You say this bricklayer is angry with the Chinese for raising him such luscious grapes for almost nothing; and yet while he is paying money out of one pocket to get them, he is paying money out of the other pocket to keep them from coming? What does it mean?"

Michael. "I can only tell you that such will be the plan on which a large part of the activity of labor organizations will be directed in the future. For example, the only time that the family of this bricklayer whom we are now visiting really suffered for the necessaries of life was last winter. The suffering happened in this way: The miners in the interior of Pennsylvania and along the Alleghany Mountains, where most all the coal for future use is to come from, had a quarrel with their employers about their wages, and refused to work. Many thousand members of other labor organizations, among them this very bricklayer, paid every shilling they could spare from their wages to support the miners, and enable them to hold out against their employers. The consequence was that coal enough was not mined to supply the whole population, and the price was so high that this brick layer could not buy enough to keep his children warm. Just as he pays money out of one pocket to buy grapes, and out of the other pocket to keep them from coming, so he contributed money out of one pocket to keep miners from digging coal, and, in consequence, did not have money enough in the other pocket to buy coal with."

Deacon. "But, surely, intelligent, God-fearing men will rise to point out to these deluded Knights the folly of their action and the fallacies of their arguments?"

Michael. "Perhaps so. But many other learned men will rise and tell the Knights that they have studied all history; that the laborers are very much abused men, and are just learning a little about their rights; and will do all they can to make them discontented with their lot, and encourage them in all the foolish devices by which they are working their own hurt."

Deacon. "If common-sense is to disappear from mankind in this way, what is to become of them? Cannot you let me see another hundred years ahead?"

But our time is now up, and we are not allowed to listen further to the conversation.

XIII.
THE ACCOUNT CURRENT.

Every man of business must keep an account of his receipts and expenditures in order to learn whether he is gaining or losing by the various enterprises in which he engages. When, tracing out the effect of any policy, he finds a greater outgo than income, he knows that he is losing; and in the opposite case he knows that he is making a profit. This is what every one of us should do when possible, in order to learn whether we gain or lose by our enterprises. Hence I propose that the laboring classes at large shall keep an account current of their gains and losses by the labor movement, because in that way, and in no other, can they learn how they stand. They want to gain benefits which will counterbalance all their expenditures, and it is only by putting down the losses and gains that they can decide whether they are succeeding.

I am now going to present one side of such an account current to the best of my ability. I do not pretend that it is a perfect account, and therefore I desire the reader to correct it wherever he finds it wrong. The principal items of debit have been given in the preceding chapters, though not always stated fully in amounts. When they are all collected the account may be made out in the form which I am now going to give.

I must also disclaim any special knowledge of the exact amounts which should be charged. Of course, such evils as we have shown to flow from certain phases of the labor movement do not admit of exact measurement in dollars, and therefore the amount of the damage will be differently estimated by different men. If the reader thinks I have either underestimated or overestimated the money values, he is at perfect liberty to correct them. All I ask is, that he will carefully weigh the matter, put down the items just as he thinks they ought to stand, and draw his own conclusions.

THE LABOR MOVEMENT IN ACCOUNT WITH THE LABORING MAN.

Dr.

To amounts contributed to support strikers upon the Missouri Pacific road, and to stop the trains on that road from bringing coal, leather, beef, and many other necessaries of life to the laboring men in Eastern cities $50,000

To higher prices which the laborers of St. Louis had to pay for coal in consequence of the above stoppage   40,000

Damages suffered by twenty thousand laborers who could no longer send their children to school in consequence of the loss of employment through the strike; damages assessed at three dollars for each family thus suffering 60,000

To ten millions of laborers having to pay on the average one cent more for a pair of shoes in consequence of the same strike   100,000

Assessments to support strike of coal-miners in Pennsylvania   Unknown

Increased price which laborers had to pay for coal in consequence of said strike, amounting to twenty cents each for five hundred thou sand families   100,000

Contributions to support strikers on the Third Avenue Railroad in New York city   20,000

Loss of time suffered by twenty thousand laborers who wanted to ride on that road and could not; assessed at fifty cents each   10,000

Wear and tear of shoe leather suffered by these same people because they had to walk, at ten cents each   2000

Privation and suffering undergone by three thousand employees deprived
of employment by the said strike at $50 each   150,000

Etc., etc., etc.

I see that, in making out this account, I have undertaken a task which is far
beyond my powers. I cannot possibly enumerate the thousands of cases in which
large bodies of working people have been ordered away from their employment,
or found their establishments boycotted since the beginning of 1886. These strikes
have every one caused privation and suffering to scores, hundreds, or thousands of
people. They have also caused indirect loss to all laborers in the country through
their having to pay higher prices for the necessaries of life. They have also done
injury to the rising generation of little children of laborers, whose parents could
no longer give them the necessary quantity of wholesome food and send them to
school to be educated. They have deprived thousands of poor seamstresses of regular employment because those who employ them fear to do so, owing to the de-
rangement of business caused by the labor movement

Nor is the end yet reached. Next winter the distress thus caused will be yet
more severely felt; and it may be that the poorer classes in our cities will suffer
from want of employment, and hence of food and fire as they have never before
suffered in our time. All who have carefully studied the preceding talks will see
that it is impossible for business to be deranged as it has been without every laborer
in the land suffering. And why all this? Because a large body of laborers in regular
employment, railway employees, operatives in factories, drivers and conductors of
street cars, and men engaged in nearly every branch of industry, with astonishing unwisdom, gave up their personal liberty, and pledged themselves to abandon
their employment and see their families suffer whenever their irresponsible leaders
chose to give the order. I can scarcely recall anything in human history so unwise as
this. We read of men having inflicted great damage upon their neighbors and upon
their enemies; but I hardly know where we should look for an instance in which
men have thus made war upon themselves and upon their own means of living, by
joining together in a movement to stop each other from manufacturing the neces-

saries of life and from earning the wages necessary to the support of their families. That any movement conceived in such folly can lead to good is contrary to reason and sound sense.

But, before winding up the account, we should ascertain what is to be put down on the credit side. I confess I find it difficult to do this, because I cannot think of anything belonging on the credit side which it would not seem almost ridiculous to put down. The laborers have had several pages of good advice from Mr. Powderly, which they may estimate at one hundred dollars per word. They have had the pleasure of being patted on the back by scheming politicians desirous of buying their votes by pandering to their folly. I would like to know just at what price they value this gratification. Certain of their leaders have had the satisfaction of showing their power by ordering thousands of men to quit their employment at a moment's notice, without reason. That any general good has been done I am quite unable to conceive.

I fancy I hear a Knight of Labor replying to this: You mistake the object of our order, if you suppose it to be the encouragement of strikes and boycotts. The fact is the contrary. One of our great objects is to do away with the necessity for either strikes or boycotts ; and you should give us credit for whatever good we may thus attain.

I am going to consider the platform and work of the Knights of Labor in the next two talks. At present I remind you that the foregoing current account is made out in the name of labor organizations in general, and not in that of the Knights of Labor in particular. At the same time I have a word to say in reply to the foregoing remark. Not long since I read an article by a supporter of the labor movement, in which he complains that people talked about and condemned this movement, when they really knew nothing about the objects of the movement, and had never read the platform of the Knights of Labor.

In reply to all this I make a statement which may sound almost paradoxical—to wit, that it is not at all necessary, in discussing this subject, to inquire what the objects of the labor movement are. So far as I have seen, the objects of all socialistic movements are most excellent, and I freely admit that the same is true of your objects. But it is not the objects which we are concerned with, but practical results. If any movement is productive of bad results, we should condemn it, no matter how pure and philanthropic the motives of its promoters may be.

Your order, and perhaps other labor organizations, want to make radical changes in the constitution of society. As a matter of fact your efforts have done and are doing untold harm and very little good. The activity and power of the Knights of Labor have so far been directed towards the promotion and not towards the suppression of strikes, and it was their assemblies which introduced the boycott into this country. You know that all the disturbances which now threaten the industries of the country, and which are going to be productive of such unheard-of distress among all laboring classes next winter, have been, to a great extent, engineered and carried through by assemblies and leaders of the Knights of Labor. This plain fact is an answer to every objection that can be made.

XIV.
A TALK TO A KNIGHT OF LABOR.

Talking to a Knight of Labor, I would say: A great many men are now talking to you, at you, and about you. These talkers consider you from two quite distinct points of view. One class look upon you as little children in wisdom, whose favor is to be gained, not by telling you what is true, but by telling you what they think it is most agreeable to you to hear. They pat you on the back, tell you what smart little boys you are, and offer you candy in order that you may think well of them and vote for them. They say it is of no use to reason with you, or do anything but humor and cajole you. The other class look upon you as mature men of sense, animated by motives as high as those which move men in general, ready to do what is for the greatest good to the greatest number; but not so thoroughly trained in history, technology, finance, and other branches of knowledge that you have all the facts which ought to guide you at your finger ends. If you have read my preceding chapters you will see that I belong to this second class; and you will bear me witness that I never offered you a single stick of candy to vote for me. I now want to talk to you very plainly about your platform, your work, and your objects.

Your platform begins by claiming that "the alarming development and aggressiveness of great capitalists and corporations, unless checked, will inevitably lead to the pauperization and hopeless degradation of the toiling masses," and then adds: "It is imperative, if we desire to enjoy the full blessings of life, that a check be placed upon unjust accumulation and the power for evil of aggregated wealth." You yourselves are supposed to belong to these "toiling masses" whom pauperization and hopeless degradation are staring in the face. Now I submit that to talk of men who contribute as much time and money as you do to printing, publishing, holding meetings, and supporting public speakers, strikers, and unemployed members, being pauperized and degraded, is a contradiction in terms. It is like a body of sturdy men walking through the streets and crying aloud: "We are sick and prisoners, and so weak from starvation that we can scarcely speak or move." Men who are really pauperized and degraded cannot combine as you have done, and cannot raise the moneys which your order commands. You will see the contrast in its strongest light by inquiring how it comes that you are so successful in your efforts.

Two or three hundred years ago the formation of any such organization as yours would have been utterly out of the question; and that for two reasons. In the first place, the laws did not recognize the equal right of men of all classes to combine together for promoting their objects. Had it then been attempted to form an order of the Knights of Labor for the purpose of doing what you have done in this country, the leaders would have been brought into court and punished by fine or imprisonment. It is because our ideas of human rights and human liberties have advanced, and have found expression in our laws and political institutions, that you are now allowed to become Knights of Labor at all.

In the next place, the formation of such an order in former times was impossible because laboring men could not possibly spare the time, money, or thought to engage in such business. In order to make a bare living they had to work from twelve to sixteen hours a day. Not only grown people had to work, but as soon as a child acquired the muscular ability to perform any regular labor it had to help earn a living, instead of going to school as your children do. The result of this was that people had neither the time nor the ability to educate themselves into our modern ideas. After working twelve or sixteen hours children were too tired to learn, and grown people were too tired to think. Every hour which a laborer gave to the formation or management of a great organization would have been so much out of his means of living.

This is no longer the case. Evidently when laborers can make a living with from eight to twelve hours' work, can spare the time, the money, and the thought to engage in organizing, and can let their children go to the public schools, there has been a very great change in their condition. Now let me ask you why this change. I want you to ask it yourself and to ask all your fellow-knights, and not to be satisfied until you get an answer which is perfectly satisfactory to you.

I will tell you my answer. It has all been done by capital, capitalists, and corporations. You are now able to make a living with such comparative ease through the introduction of machinery, and the building of railroads to make and bring within reach of you the necessaries of life. In modern society capital means railroads, steamboats, and machinery. And capitalists mean the men who know how to build railroads and steamboats and run machinery, and who are willing to apply their wealth-producing powers to such enterprises. To say that such men and such things lead to your pauperization is like saying that the bread you eat leads to starvation, and that the house you are in is the cause of your exposure to the weather. It is as near to a contradiction in terms as anything well can be.

You probably know that the great question which has divided men during the last two hundred years is whether you, the laboring masses, can safely be trusted to guide your own destinies. The old conservative party thinks you cannot. It says that the management of public affairs requires the highest wisdom, and as you do not possess this wisdom you should not be allowed to exercise power. The other side claims that though great wisdom is required in public affairs, it is not necessary to the exercise of power, because men who are not wise themselves may choose wiser men to act for them.

It seems to me that the present is the most critical time the world has ever seen for these two theories to be tried. There is nothing in history to correspond to the improvement in the laboring man's condition; I mean the condition of that class of laborers who join the Knights, during the last twenty years. For the first time in the history of the world millions of toiling laborers have been able to collect hundreds of thousands—I suppose, indeed, millions—of dollars, for the purpose of giving effect to their views of society and government. Thus the conservative and progressive parties have before them the very men whom they have been disputing about, just getting ready to act, and the whole question is whether they will use their newly acquired power wisely or foolishly. I have no hesitation in saying that if you use it as indicated in your platform, and as it has already been used, you will use it foolishly and in a way that will ultimately lead to its loss and to your own degradation. Let us see if this is not true.

In the first place, if you read the preceding chapters carefully, and study out the conditions on which your welfare depends, you will see as plain as day that you have been engaged in attacking the very instrumentalities which have given you the power you now wield. It is capital, as embodied in railways and machinery, which has given you all these benefits, with the power they bring, and capital is one of the main objects which you attack. Perhaps you may say that it is not the capital itself, but the owners of it, which you attack. But if you will read carefully what I have said you will see that the owners are nothing more than the managers of the capital, and that, if you do not allow them the privilege of managing the capital they have acquired, the capital itself will disappear with them.

But this is not the only foolish thing you are doing. You are rejecting something which more than anything else makes life worth living, and which has cost your forefathers more toil and bloodshed than anything else in the world—namely, individual liberty. The other day a mechanic was asked why he engaged in the strike when he was perfectly satisfied with his employer and when the strike would probably subject his wife and children to distress. He replied that he was ordered to do so, and must obey at whatever cost. If asked to justify his course, he would probably have said that he had voluntarily given up his own individual rights for what he supposed to be the benefit of his class.

Now what I wish to impress upon you is this—that the position of a man who thus gives up his individual liberty is worse than the position of the meanest subject of the greatest tyrant of modern times. When a man receives the order, "Do not go to work to-day," it is the same to him whether it comes from a czar, a satrap, or a master workman. Our laws do not even recognize the right of a man to sell himself in slavery, and, except as a matter of sentiment and feeling, this giving up of liberty is not a whit better than an involuntary slavery.

You not only surrender your own natural rights, but you encroach upon the rights of such of your fellow-laborers as will not or cannot join your ranks in the most cruel manner. If there is any one natural right of humanity which the most heartless tyrant never dared to deny it is that of every man to make an honest living in his own way, by any reputable pursuit he chooses to follow. But one great object of labor organization is to prevent any skilled laborer from making "a living 'unless he will join a labor union. The man may not be able to earn union wages; he may have such 8 sense of his rights that he will not become the subject of a tyranny; he may not be willing to contribute money for the support of strikers; he may have a family of helpless children dependent on him for support. In every case your members are required to refuse to work with him, and to do all in their power not only to secure his pauperization and degradation, but the starvation of himself and his race. Never was a tyrant, never was a public enemy, seldom was an invading army, engaged in greater cruelty than this.

XV.
ANOTHER TALK TO A KNIGHT OF LABOR.

I esteem it the duty of a good citizen to promote every movement that is good, and to oppose every movement that is bad in its effects. Most great movements like that which you are now inaugurating have a good object, but, as I have already said, it does not follow that, because the object is good, therefore the effect will be good. The efforts of large bodies of men like yours are very apt to be productive of effects the very opposite of those which it is desired to attain. It is also the case that men do not always act in accordance with their avowed principles. I therefore ask leave once more to call your attention to some utterances in your platform. I find the first object at which you aim to be expressed in the following words:

I. "To make industrial and moral worth, not wealth, the true standard of individual and national greatness."

I think this looks in the right direction. True, it implies that wealth is something entirely disconnected from either industrial or moral worth, and if you have carefully read the preceding chapters you will see that this is a mistake. But I do not now insist upon this point. The great question I have now to put to you is this: What does your order of Knights of Labor do to promote industrial worth? To answer this question we must inquire what industrial worth is and how it is to be measured.

It is very clear to me that industrial worth is to be measured by the amount of good which a man does by his labor, bodily or mental. For example: The industrial worth of a bricklayer is to be estimated by the number and quality of the buildings, the walls of which he erects. The industrial worth of the miner is measured by the quantity of coal which he gets out of the ground. The industrial worth of the engine-driver is determined by the effectiveness with which he performs his duty, and the certainty and safety with which he brings his train into the station at the appointed time. In a word, the industrial worth of every man is measured by the products of his labor, and the more useful these products the greater is his worth.

If, then, you really held industrial worth to be one of the great standards of individual and national greatness, and if you acted consistently with this view, you would do all you could to increase this worth by increasing the products of every man's labor. You would discourage the eight-hour movement, because it is perfectly clear that the industrial worth of a man who only works eight hours is less than that of a man who works ten hours. You would oppose all the regulations of labor unions which require their members to refuse to work with men who do not belong to the union. You would oppose strikes, because a man on strike has no industrial worth at all. You would encourage the boys now growing up in idleness to learn trades. You would do a great many other good things to promote industrial worth in the community at large.

If you were seriously attempting to carry out these objects I should so far heartily sympathize with you. But are you really doing so? I think not. At least I never heard of any assembly of Knights of Labor opposing any of the restrictive rules of the trades-unions or trying in any way to increase the industrial worth of its members.

Now, when any person wants the public to adopt his principles, the very first step is to show that he believes in them himself. Hence you cannot expect to take any step towards making industrial worth a standard of greatness so long as your acts show that you yourselves place so low an estimate upon your own industrial worth.

I am very sorry for this. I think every man ought to be proud of his work. He benefits his fellow-men by his work, and he ought to be proud of rendering that benefit. I may be mistaken, and if I am I shall want to be corrected, but I fear that very few skilled laborers at the present time are proud of their work. This ought not to be. It seems to me that every man who does good work should take the same delight in it that authors take in writing books, and merchants in directing commerce. I remember that when a boy of fourteen I made a clock-reel, an instrument to wind yarn upon, which snapped a spring once in forty turns to show that a knot had been wound. I do not think I have ever done anything since of which I was prouder than of having made that clock-reel. I mention this merely to show that an ordinary boy, if not a man, can be proud of doing a very simple job.

If I am right in thinking that you do not take pride in your work, then there is certainly something wrong. But I do not by any means wish to imply that the fault is all, or principally, on your side. The real fault is to be found in the theories which run through society. You have so long and often been told by word and action that you are condemned to a hard fate; that other men reap the fruits of your labor; and that labor itself is a mark of degradation, that although you would rather not believe these things, you cannot help accepting them as in some sort a necessary result of the prevailing opinion of labor. Hence the first plank in your platform, which I have just quoted, is not a theory which you believe and act upon, so much as it is a theory which you would like to have believed and acted upon, if society only took the same view of the case.

I also fear that labor organizations have had a bad effect in making the workman underestimate the value of his labor, and look upon it as pure drudgery. How could it be otherwise when all the rules and regulations of such organizations imply that the greater the quantity of work done by its members or by others, the worse it is for them? Now, no man can be proud of that which it is undesirable to do. Hence the first step towards the better state of things called for in your platform is to get rid of the theory that real industrial worth is something to be discouraged, and to adopt the theory that it is something to be promoted.

The second object at which you aim is also so good that I shall here quote it in full:

II. "To secure to the workers the full enjoyment of the wealth they create; sufficient leisure in which to develop their moral and social faculties; all of the benefits of recreation and pleasure of association; in a word, to enable them to share in the gains and honors of advancing civilization."

I say this is an excellent object. The way to attain it is to increase the industrial worth of the laborer by training every boy who has the skill to learn a trade into a good workman, so that there shall be plenty of everything for everybody's use.

There are many other good things in your platform. But there are at least two things which are so bad as to more than offset any good which could be possibly done by an organization like yours.

One of your demands is for an issue of government paper money. Now, if there is any one instrumentality invented by Satan to cheat the laborer out of his earnings, it is what is called "fiat money." It cheats him because it continually pretends to pay more than it really does pay. He agrees to work for "dollars," and when he gets his dollars they are not real money at all, only little paper pictures stamped "one dollar "by Congress.

You may ask, If one of them will buy me as much as a gold dollar, why is it not just as good as a gold dollar? I answer it would be as good if it were redeemable in a gold dollar; but the supporters of fiat money do not want it so redeemed. Now all history and reason show that unless an issue of this kind of money is greatly restricted, more restricted, indeed, than a believer in it would admit of, it is sure to depreciate, and no longer to buy a dollar's worth. The more it depreciates the more anxious people are to get it, and the more anxious they are to get rid of it when they get it, and the result of this is a continual increase in the price of everything we eat, drink, and wear. It is hard to imagine what labor organizations could have proposed worse for themselves than this. It is like petitioning Congress to allow them to be cheated out of their wages.

Yet another plank which shows as little practical wisdom is that which demands the purchase of all telegraphs and railroads by the government. If you had stopped at telegraphs it would not have been so bad, because the management of a telegraph system is not so complex a matter as that of a railroad system, and, besides, private corporations have not managed our telegraphs so well as they have the railroads. But to ask that the government shall take possession of the railroads and run them shows a woful lack of practical knowledge. Such a demand could never have been proposed by any one having an intimate knowledge of the way in which government business is managed. It is most fortunate for the laboring man that there is so little chance for carrying out this plank of your platform.

XVI.
HOW CAN ALL GET BETTER WAGES!

All of us want to earn higher wages and are trying to do so. It is a good thing for all of us that we should try to do so, because, if we go about it in the right way, we shall benefit other people as well as ourselves by earning higher wages. The right way to get better wages is to render more and better services to our fellow-men, and thus induce them to pay us more for our services.

But what are the real wages we are trying to earn? The common answer will be; wages are so many dollars and cents per day or week. This answer is perfectly correct, so far as the receipts of money are concerned. We are all working to get dollars. But having got the dollars, are our wants then supplied? By no means. We cannot eat the dollars nor sleep upon them, nor hold them over our heads to protect us from the sun and rain, nor put them to any useful purpose whatever. Then why do we care for them at all? Because with them we buy the things we want—food, clothing, and shelter. The real wages which we earn in the course of the year are, not dollars, but so many suits of clothes, the privilege of living in a certain house, and so many barrels of flour, meal, and pork. These, and these alone, are the real wages; the dollars are the mere symbols which we use to get our real wages.

You will reply to this: "Very true, but the more dollars I earn the more and better food and clothing I can buy for myself and my family."

Here I join issue with you. It does not follow that you can get more of the necessaries of life whenever you earn more money in the course of the year. If prices rise in the same proportion with your wages then you gain nothing. The man who gets double wages and has to pay double prices for everything he gets is no better off than before. The real problem of getting higher wages is either to earn more money without making prices any higher, or to adopt such a policy that the prices of the necessaries of life shall be lower, without people in general earning any less wages. Either of these results will amount to an increase of wages.

But you may think that it is quite exceptional if more wages do not buy more food. To see how far this is true, let us climb up to our old standpoint and look once more at the interests of the country at large.

The organization of the Knights of Labor has one very wise and liberal feature, in that it recognizes all men who work for their living as being laborers, and therefore makes them eligible to its ranks. If I am rightly informed, gentlemen of leisure, capitalists, great managers and employers of labor, and liquor dealers, are the only classes who are deemed ineligible. These form a very small fraction of the adult population. I call attention to this fact because it enables us to agree that the laborers, whose interests I have all along been considering in these talks, form, with their families and dependants, nearly the whole of the population.

A very little consideration will show us that they do the larger part of the eating and wearing out of clothes, and occupy most of the houses. The richest man in the country eats little more beef or flour than the day laborer, and he probably eats less corn-meal and pork. He does not wear out much more clothing. For, although he spends more money in clothes, he does not wear them until they are used up, but soon passes them over to some poorer man, to be worn out by him. He does, indeed, live in a much bigger house than the poor man, and has much more costly furniture, and a greater variety of pictures and books. It is only in this way that he consumes much more of the good things of life than the poor man does.

Now a very little thought will show you that it is physically and mathematically impossible that higher wages should enable the great masses of people of the country to get more or better food or clothes, unless more or better food and clothes are made. Doubling the wages of farm hands will not increase the crop. Increasing the wages of operators will not add anything to the horse-power of the engine, and so on through the list. "What, then, would be the consequence if everybody could, from and after January 1, next, have his weekly wages exactly doubled? The result would be that everything he wanted to buy would be just twice as dear as before. It would have to be so, because it is mathematically and physically impossible that everybody should be able to buy more things than he did before. He cannot buy more than are made, and no more are made than before. True, the rise of prices might not occur immediately. There might be a few days, weeks, or months, during which everybody could buy more flour, beef, and clothing with the increased wages. But, in so doing, we would be merely drawing upon the stock in hand of these articles which is stored away in the great warehouses, and the result would be a future scarcity, which again would more than double the prices.

You reply to this: "But we do not want a policy which doubles everybody's wages. We do not want the rich man, the capitalist, the great managers, to have any larger incomes than before. Now, suppose we could adopt a policy which would leave their incomes untouched, and only increase those of the laboring masses; what then?"

The answer to this I have already given in Chapter IV. I there pointed out that no rise in price diminishes the consumption of the necessaries of life by the rich. The latter consume just as much flour, beef, and clothes when the prices go up as they did before. Therefore it would still be mathematically impossible for the poorer classes to buy any more of these necessaries than they did before, no matter how much you increased their wages.

Do I mean, then, to say that if the carpenters all got double wages they could not buy more than before? Not at all. If carpenters had their wages increased, while all other laboring men got the same wages, it is quite true that the carpenters would be able to buy and consume nearly twice as much of the necessaries of life. But what would be the consequence? With no increase of production there would be just so much less of the necessaries of life for all other laborers, and thus all the other laborers would suffer more or less by the carpenters earning higher wages. Prices would be higher, while the wages would be the same as before.

In what precedes I have talked as if it were a very simple and easy matter to get an increase of money wages. This is a wrong notion, because the amount of money which any person or corporation can pay in wages is limited by its or his means of payment. If a factory can produce and sell fifty thousand dollars' worth of cloth in a year, then $50,000 is the sum total which it could possibly pay out to employees of all kinds in the course of any year. It can, perhaps, pay one half this sum to its own operatives. A portion of the other half will be paid for material, such as wool or cotton, and the owners of this material can pay just that much and no more in wages for producing more cotton and cloth. Another portion will be paid to its stockholders and managers, and these men will then have just so much to pay directly or indirectly in wages to those who supply them with the necessaries of life.

Suppose, then, that the factory is compelled to pay higher wages. Then it must either lessen its force or it must charge a higher price for its products. In the latter case it will be bad for everybody who has to buy cloth, especially for laborers. In fact, the chances are that fewer people will buy the cloth, and thus the result will be, in the end, a diminution of production. What is true of this factory is true all the way through society. All other conditions being the same, one class cannot get an increase in money wages except at the expense of other classes. Please remember that I say, "all other conditions being equal." If with an increase of wages the laborer makes a better article than before, or a kind of article that serves a better purpose, then his increase of wages will not be at anybody's expense. But if everything he does is to go on just in the same way as before, the only result will be that everybody who has to buy the things he makes will have to pay more for them.

The inevitable conclusion is that, taking the laboring classes at large, and considering their general condition, that condition cannot be improved by mere increase of wages, unless larger and better houses are built for them to live in, better food obtained for them to eat, nicer clothes made for them to wear, better beds made for them to sleep on. The country at large must make so many hair mattresses and soft blankets that there shall be enough to go all round, supplying the poor as well as the rich. We must build plenty of houses, so that everybody shall have plenty of house-room. This requires that we shall make more bricks, get more timber, and employ more men in learning how to build houses. Inventors must devise improved machinery for making furniture, so that our factories shall turn it out in such quantities that there shall be cushioned chairs for everybody to sit upon, and handsome china plates for everybody to eat off of.

Conversely, if all these improvements are made in production we are sure to get the advantage of them, no matter whether our wages are increased or not. The good things will all go begging rather than remain year after year unsold, and will be sure to find purchasers.

If the Knights of Labor will turn the great power of their organization towards the stir-ring-up of everybody to carry out these objects, by inducing young boys to learn all sorts of trades, instead of idling about the streets, by encouraging rich men to invest their money in machinery, and by insuring everybody who shall take part in the enterprise the secure enjoyment of all his rights, then they will render a benefit to themselves and their fellow-laborers of the country and of the world.

XVII.
CHEAP LABOR AND ITS EFFECTS.

If the reader has carefully studied the preceding chapters he will see that there must be something wrong in the theories on which labor organizations are generally based. At the same time it may seem to him that every effort which the labor movement is engaged in is a perfectly natural result of sound reasoning. Such being the case, the thinking man who desires to have none but correct theories will not be satisfied with the mere suspicion that the labor theories are wrong. He may say to me: "What you have said seems quite plausible. At the same time the course of thought by which I have been led to favor the labor movement seems to me still more plausible; at least I do not see anything wrong in it. I feel, therefore, a certain amount of confusion and doubt on the subject, because two ways of looking at the subject, both of which seem sound, lead to contradictory results."

I now have to clear up this difficulty by showing what is wrong in the popular theories on which the labor movement is based. To the common mind some of these theories look so plain and simple that they cannot be doubted, while all seem to have much in their favor; yet I hope to show you that they are entirely unsound. I shall try to put these principles in the clearest light, so that every promoter of the labor movement will recognize them as being the embodiment of his own ideas, and as being what he would himself my if called upon to defend his position. I state them as follows :

Firstly, when one man competes with another by underselling him in the market or working for lower wages than the latter gets, you hold that he does him an injury by lessening the demand for his goods or his labor. For example, bricklayers in a certain town are getting $4 per day. A half-dozen bricklayers come from some other city and offer to work for $2 per day. You think that they injure the home bricklayers who have been getting the higher wages, by depressing their wages either to $2 a day or to some intermediate point, say $3 or $3.50.

Secondly, carrying out this principle, you claim that unlimited competition is an evil, in that men who compete with each other to furnish labor or goods at the lowest price that they are able to, injure each other, and hence injure society at large. Hence you want to limit competition.

Thirdly, if called upon to defend these principles you would probably say that the man who worked more cheaply than another took work from that other man.

I might ask you, why so? If one man is drinking water out of a river and two or three other men come and drink water from the same river, they do not take water from the first man, because there is enough for all of them and a thousand times more.

You would probably reply to this, that although there is water enough in the river for everybody and a thousand times over, there is not work enough in the country, even for the people already in it, and, therefore, to get a parallel I ought to take a case where there is not waterenough to go around. Then, of course, the three new men would take water from the first. You would claim in the same way that competing laborers took work from each other.

Now I wish to point out to you that these principles are, to a great extent, fallacious. When I say that they are fallacious I do not mean that they are all the reverse of truth, as if they had claimed that black was white and white was black. What I mean is that they are true only to a limited extent, and on one side, as it were, and that it is not this true side of them which is put into practice.

To begin with the third principle. I think you can see without doubt that you are wrong in thinking that the work to be done is limited. Millions of farmers in the Western states and territories are calling loudly for railways to be extended to their neighborhood in order that they may send their products to market and get back the manufactures which they are in need of. Thirty millions of people within these United States want their houses improved. They would like to have better walls, and roofs that would never leak, and new stoves or furnaces to warm them in winter. That same number of people want newer and whiter table-cloths, warmer and nicer clothing, better beds, the means of sending their children to school in winter, books and papers for them to read, and, indeed, an unlimited supply of good things of all kinds. You know perfectly well that all these things require labor to produce them, and that the reason that everybody is in want of them is that all the labor of the country is not sufficient to supply them, unless people do more work than they are accustomed to.

If you will follow up this train of thought by spending some five minutes in thinking of everything you would like to have, and five minutes more in thinking of everything your neighbor would like to have, and then calculate how much labor it would take to supply all these wants, you will see that the amount of work to be done is really unlimited.

Why is there any obstacle to this work being done? Why has not everybody got all the work he wants? The answer is: People have not money enough to pay for it. Ah! Here is the rub. There is work enough to be done, but people have not the money to pay for it. If you are a carpenter and earn $3 a day for 250 days in the year you have just $750 to buy the products of other people's labor with, and this makes up all the wages you can pay to others, Thus we reach the first great modification which your principle requires: It is not the work to be done which is limited, but it is the wages which people can afford to pay for that work. And here you must not forget what I pointed out in a preceding chapter, that the real wages are not the money, but what the laborer buys with the money.

Let us now go back to our first example. A hundred bricklayers are at work in a town at $4 a day. Ten new ones come in and offer to lay bricks at $2 a day. Will not the wages of the hundred bricklayers then be depressed? Are people going to pay $4 a day for work when they can get it done for $2 a day? Before we can fully answer this question we must look carefully into the conditions. Perhaps the ten new bricklayers can only do the work of five old ones. In this case they will not really be any cheaper than the old ones, and will not injuriously compete with them. If they really do a full day's work they would be fools to work for $2 per day when they could get almost $4. But, to get the strongest possible case for your principle, suppose they are just such fools, or, if you choose, such philanthropists, that they don't want more than $2 per day. Then many people will be anxious to get their services. To make the case as strong as possible, suppose some of the master builders who have been paying the highest wages discharge ten of their men and take the new men in their places. What will be the result?

To answer this question we must remember that before the ten cheap men came there were in the town so many people in want of houses being built that they were willing to give $4 per day to a hundred bricklayers. That is, they would rather pay these high wages than not have their work done. No doubt they would all like to have their work done at half price, but they cannot possibly get it so done, because there are only ten cheap men, whereas a hundred are wanted to do the work. The latter is worth just as much as it was before the cheap men came, so that the ninety bricklayers who were not discharged may still command $4 per day.

But what will the ten men who are discharged do? I answer, when there are a number of men willing to give $4 per day for bricklayers there are always a number of others who think they cannot afford to have their bricklaying done at that price, but who would be willing to pay some lower price, say $3.75. The ten discharged men will have no trouble in getting work at these wages.

Thus it is perfectly true that the wages of the bricklayers are, on the average, slightly depressed by the introduction of the ten new men. We may suppose that in the long run the other ninety will have to submit to the same reduction, and get only $3.75 instead of $4. Up to this point you are quite right in saying that the competition of new and cheap men will depress the wages of others to a certain extent. You are wrong in supposing it would depress them to any wages the new men choose to work for. If the latter demanded the highest wages they could get, then all would be employed at $3.75 per day.

If this were the end of the matter then your principle would be sounder than it is, but it is not the end of the matter. I think, however, this is about as far as we can go without stopping to rest, so let us take a breathing-spell before showing what the end of the matter is.

XVIII.
THE SAME SUBJECT CONTINUED.

In order to continue the examination which we started in the last chapter, it is necessary to explain a somewhat intricate principle on which the whole result turns.

Let us suppose that there are ten men, James, John, William, Peter, etc., who are working in co-operation with each other, and are trying to promote each other's interests as well as their own, so as to do, on the whole, what is best for all ten of them.

A party comes to them and proposes that they shall engage with him in some enterprise, no matter what, in which each man shall take a different part. On calculating the profit and loss to be expected, they find that Peter will lose three cents while the nine others will gain one cent each. Peter does not want to lose three cents, and they do not want him to lose it, so they all say, "It is too bad if we, to make one cent each, cause Peter to lose three cents. Therefore we will reject this man's proposal."

Next day another man comes and offers employment under which John would lose three cents while all the rest would gain one cent each as before. They reject this proposal for the same reason. So they go on from day to day rejecting all proposals by which any one of their number shall lose.

Then an offer is made them by which Peter would gain three cents while the other nine would lose but one cent each. "It will be very nice for Peter to gain three cents," they all say, "and what do we care for one cent. Let us accept this proposal for Peter's sake. By tomorrow we shall have an offer by which William shall gain three cents, and next day one by which John shall gain three cents, and so on. We will accept all these offers, and thus we shall all get the advantages of the three cents while nobody will lose more than one cent at a time."

Now it needs no high mathematics to see that these ten men have been rejecting the offers which, on the whole, would have been advantageous to them, considered as a single body, and accepting disadvantageous offers. They have suffered nine cents to be lost for every three they have gained because, on each occasion, they had in view the interest of the one gainer and overlooked that of the nine losers. Thus they rejected chances of gaining a sum total of six cents and accept chances which led to a loss of six cents.

This is what men are always doing, and always proposing to do in their action upon economic questions. We may take the preceding ten men to represent so many classes of the leading laborers; say railroad employees, bricklayers, carpenters, tailors, shoemakers, farmers, factory hands, furniture-makers, etc. Whenever any measure is proposed by which some one of these trades may lose a little, they get the others to oppose it, no matter whether the others gain or not. When some one trade has a chance to gain it gets the others to accept, no matter if they are all to lose. As a familiar example, take the case of the strike. When the street-car drivers all struck the laborers of other trades contributed money to support them, and still others suffered for want of cars to ride in. The sum total of the loss, even to the laboring classes alone, was in all cases greater than the sum total of the gain.

Nothing can happen in the commercial world which will not be more or less to the disadvantage of somebody. If there is a good crop of wheat, the men who are holding wheat to sell are losers for the time being. When machinery is introduced to do the work of laborers, the laborers whose work they take are losers for the time being. If a man stops buying luxuries in order to save money to buy a house, the people who have been making him those luxuries are for the time being at a disadvantage. If cheap labor from another state is introduced, the laborers whose places are taken are at a temporary disadvantage. If we should attempt to stop all such disadvantages we should have to stop all improvements in production, and, in fact, perhaps, have to lapse back into barbarism.

A very simple common-sense rule will tell us whether a policy thus temporarily disadvantageous should or should not be persisted in. What we have to do is not merely to consider the persons who are for the time at a disadvantage, but the sum total of interests of the whole community, future as well as present. If a policy which leads to a diminution of twenty-five cents per day in the wages of bricklayers during a whole season will result in a permanent advantage to all the rest of the community, not only during the season, but in the future, it would be folly to reject it. On this principle let us count up the advantages and disadvantages of the state of things described in our last chapter.

We there supposed ten cheap-working bricklayers to come into a city where one hundred men had been previously employed at that trade at $4 per day. We showed that the first effect of this would be that which everybody plainly sees, that wages would be depressed by the competition. If the one hundred bricklayers were determined not to work for less than $4 per day, ten of them would have to be thrown out of employment for the time being. They would either have to wait for work, or go to some other place where they might command better wages. If, however, they were willing to submit to a reduction of wages from $4 to perhaps $3.75, then all would find employment.

Now I do not wish you for one moment to ignore the plain fact that so far as these one hundred bricklayers are, for the time being, concerned, this reduction of wages is an evil for them. But I do wish you to see, what everybody ignores, that this loss is made up by a more than equal gain for the rest of the community; just as Peter's loss of three cents was offset by a gain of one cent each to his nine fellows, so all other laborers will very soon gain exactly what the bricklayers have lost, and, later, a great deal more. To see this, all we have to do is to study out the effect of the changes.

To make this effect clear, suppose all the bricklayers are employed by a single man. Then, after wages are lowered twenty-five cents per day, that man will be making $25 per day extra profit. If he spends no more money than he would have spent had he gone on paying the highest wages, then, at the end of one hundred days, he will have $2500 extra in his bank. What will he do with this money? Throw it into the river? I trow not. Put it away in a stocking? Not if he has common-sense enough to manage a business. It is morally certain that he will either buy something with it or hire somebody to work with it. He may start a new house; and then he will want an additional force of bricklayers, tinners, plumbers, glaziers, hod-carriers, and teamsters. He will thus create an additional demand for the services of these men, and they would then get in extra wages the whole $2500, if he spent the whole of it in this way. Perhaps, however, he will spend $300 of it in buying his wife a piano, which he would not have bought otherwise. Then the music dealer will have $300 which he would not have had if wages had kept up. The music dealer will spend $50 of this sum, perhaps, in buying a new horse, which he could not have bought if he had not sold the piano, and he will send the remainder to the piano manufacturer in payment for pianos furnished, and the manufacturer will then have so much more to pay in wages to his workmen. Now, make what supposition you please respecting the manner in which the man spends his money, and you will find that every cent which the bricklayers lose in wages goes to the employment of just that much labor in other kinds of work, so that laborers as a class do not lose at all.

You may reply to this: "Let us admit that they do not lose, still they do not gain : hence this lowering of wages is not desirable, because it is only giving to one set of laborers what properly belongs to another."

This objection would be quite well founded if we were dealing only with the lowering of wages of bricklayers, regardless of the causes by which the depression was produced. But let us now go back to the beginning and consider the causes which we have supposed to lead to the depression, namely, the influx of ten cheap-working bricklayers. In consequence of the arrival of these men there are one hundred and ten bricklayers engaged in building houses instead of one hundred. The result is that ten per cent, more houses are built, and that the whole community will get their houses cheaper than they otherwise would, or will get better houses at the old prices. In either case there is a clear, permanent gain for the whole community, laborers included. Every laborer has a better house than he would have had if the cheap men had not come.

Now if we reject this clear surplus of gains over losses by driving away or keeping out these cheap bricklayers, we will do exactly what we supposed the ten men to do when they rejected a chance to gain a cent each because some one of their number would lose three cents. I do not for a moment deny that, so far as the bricklayers themselves are concerned, the loss would exceed the gain. The cheapening of their rents would not compensate them for the loss of twenty-five cents a day in wages. But next week some other chance will arise by which they will gain. A new railroad will be built which will bring them cheaper goods. A new post-office will be built, and there will be an extra demand for their labor. Some of them will die or will leave for other cities, and there will be none to take their places until their own wages are raised. In a word, they take their chances like everybody else, and good chances are sure to come as well as bad ones.

I think if you look at the facts of the case you will see that the soundness of this principle is proved by facts. Take, for example, the Chinese emigration into California. The effect of this emigration is commonly supposed to be the depression of wages on the Pacific Coast. I think, however, if you study out the matter you will find that such is not the case, and that there is no place where the industrious laborer is better off to-day than he is in California. Whatever he has lost by Chinese competition he has more than gained by the cheapening of the necessaries of life.

XIX. IS WASTE A GOOD?

In the last two talks I set forth the fallacy of the current notion that the competition of cheap labor, or "underpaid labor," was a bad thing for other labor. But this by no means exhausts the subject. There is much digging to be done at the root of the theories I have described, and I beg the reader to assist me in trying what more false doctrines we can dig up.

I have in my mind a fleet of rowboats, some pulled by one man and some by a dozen, whose crews are all trying to make their way across a wide expanse of water. But they all have a notion that in order to row in the right direction they must turn their faces towards the place they want to reach; and so they persist, whenever they get a chance, in turning the boats around and rowing in a direction they do not want to, just because they entertain this false theory.

Now there is current among us a theory which is as far wrong as the theory that a boat is rowed in the direction in which the rower's face is turned. We see it cropping out in all the speeches of labor reformers, in the resolutions of labor conventions, and in the proceedings of Congress. The theory is, in brief, that waste is a public benefit, and cheapness a public evil; that it is a bad thing for laborers when new and cheap substitutes for what they make are discovered, because there is then less demand for their labor; that the more work the laborer does the worse for himself and fellow-laborers; that it is a good thing for workmen when things are lost and destroyed, because they will then be engaged in remaking them.

As examples: The main ground on which a protective tariff has so strong a hold upon us is the doctrine that an influx of cheap goods from abroad is an evil. The oleomargarine bill was passed by both houses of Congress by a large majority, because it was believed to be a public misfortune for the people at large to be able to get butter for their bread at ten cents a pound. Of course, a great many other reasons were assigned, but the bottom reason was just that. If it had not been so cheap no one would ever have inquired whether it was a fraud or whether it was unwholesome. Our laws now prohibit the immigration of Chinese laborers, and the main reason on which they are based is that these laborers do so much work for so little money. None of the other reasons would have been thought of but for this. A very serious discussion is going on in legislatures and labor meetings about convict labor, and its competition with paid labor. The idea on which the discussion is based is that it would be a public evil to have convicts producing valuable goods at no cost to the public. It is supposed that the public will be better off if these convicts are supported in idleness than if they are made to work for the public benefit. A few weeks ago Mr. T. V. Powderly, Grand Master Workman of the Knights of Labor, was reported to have said in a speech to the glass-blowers:

"Any bottle brought into my house does not go back. I cannot smash a beer bottle, because I drink ginger ale, but the bottle never goes out alive. That is a small thing; but if ninety thousand men who get bottles were to destroy them it would make a big hole."

Whether this statement was made by Mr. Powderly or not, it voices the prevailing sentiment on the subject. Most fortunately for mankind, hardly anybody ever applies this principle in his own individual case. If all did, we should very soon be transformed into a horde of half-starved barbarians. Every sensible man tries to get things as cheaply as possible, and to make them last as long as they can be made to, whereas all organized action on this theory is directed towards making them cost as much as possible.

We may show this theory to be wrong, either by the reason of the case or the facts of the case. In the first place, if we admit it where shall we stop? If ninety thousand people make work for others by smashing all their bottles after being once used, would they not, on the same principle, benefit chairmakers if they should destroy all their chairs after using them a short time, say a month? One man could not do much in this way, but ninety thousand could make a big hole in the existing supply of chairs. What is true of the chairs would apply also to all the furniture of a house, the plates and the dishes. If ninety thousand men should break them up, after having used them a year, they would make a big hole to be filled up by labor. If a man burned down his new house after living in it a year, would it not, on the same principle, be good for the house-builders? Then would not everybody be rendering a public benefit by doing the same thing?

Of course you will reply to me that you do not carry your theory so far as this, and do not propose to run it into the ground, as I am doing. But where will you stop? If your theory is good for so little a thing as a bottle; why should it not be good for so big a thing as a house? If you claim that there is a turning-point, please tell me where it is that waste ceases to be beneficial to the public. When you have done this to your own satisfaction, I will tell you my answer. "Waste is of no benefit at all, and the theory that it is beneficial to anybody arises from not looking at all the facts of the case. Let us see what the facts all come to.

Suppose that Mr. Powderly drinks one bottle of ginger ale a day, and that the bottle is worth three cents. This will make, in round numbers, ten dollars' worth of bottles a year which he destroys. If he sold the bottles, instead of destroying them, he would have had just $10 more in his pocket at the end of the year. With that $10 he would have bought something useful to himself. By so doing he would have given just the same employment to the laborers engaged in making these useful things that he gave to the glassmakers by breaking the bottles. If he bought a pair of fine boots, as he might well do, there would have been $10 more in the pockets of the shoemaker. So all he does by destroying the bottles is to give employment to bottle-makers at the expense of shoemakers, or whatever trade makes the goods he would have bought with the money gained by selling the bottles.

Now this is a principle which comes in to all these cases. No cheapening process can diminish the sum total of the demand for labor, for the plain and simple reason that everybody to whom money is saved by such cheapening is going to employ labor, or buy the products of labor with it. This side of the case is what we are all prone to forget when we discuss the question.

Notwithstanding its absurdity, the theory in question seems to be as natural as the theory that a boat must be going in the direction in which the rower turns his face. No doubt the first time you, as a child, got into a boat and tried to row, you entertained this view, and it was only when you found that you were pulling the boat in the opposite direction that you got cured of the notion. Probably this did not take five minutes; and having once learned the falsity of your idea you never afterwards tried to put it into practice. But the great difficulty with the labor theories is that their falsity cannot be made evident without a great deal of thinking and a great deal of study; and thought and study are not properly given to the problem. The fact is, that the theory that cheap production is an evil, is remarkable not only because it is so very natural, but because it is completely disproved by all the facts of the case. Let us glance for a moment at what would have been the consequence, had it been acted upon.

Every railway that has been built comes into competition with stage-coaches, wagons, teamsters, and innkeepers, and drives them right out of business by doing the work a great deal cheaper. Therefore had the theory been carried out to its utmost extent, we should never have had any railroads.

The spinning jenny threw thousands of operatives out of employment, and caused great distress among large classes of laborers. The latter did all they could to destroy the machines ; in fact the cry, "Smash the machine!" has almost come down to our day. Had the operatives been able to have things their own way we should still be making all our cloth by hand.

The result of the theory would have been that we should now have been in the same industrial condition that our ancestors were a hundred years ago; that is, the hours of labor would have been from twelve to sixteen daily; the laborers would have had no clothing except such as their wives could spin, weave, sew, and patch; their children would have gone barefoot half the year, and been miserably shod the other half; there would have been no labor organizations, because, as I have shown, when men have to work from twelve to sixteen hours a day they have neither time nor energy to organize; the principal furniture of a laborer's cottage would have been a straw bed, hard-bottomed wooden chairs, and a plain pine table. In a word, his condition would have been one in which the laborer of the present day would not consider that life was worth living.

I have abundantly shown what, in fact, every man who has intellectual eyes can see by looking at it, that the reason why the laborer of to-day is so much better off, is that the force of circumstances have been stronger than his theory. Capitalists have persisted in building railways to bring him the products of other regions, and in making machinery to supply him with clothes and furniture; in a word, to do for him the very thing which, according to his theory, it is disadvantageous to have done. Under these circumstances I earnestly hope that labor organizations will not succeed in doing themselves irreparable damage by putting this old theory into operation. I hope the common-sense of society will prevail upon them to see that the laborer is best supplied with the necessaries of life when every man is at work at the very best wages he can get, be they high or low.

Closely associated with the policy I have pointed out is the fear that one man will get along a little faster than another. I have not so low an opinion of human nature as to believe that this fear can arise from mere jealousy. I take it that when a labor union stops one of its members from doing more work and thus earning higher wages than the others, it is because they fear the others are injured by such a course. In a word, they think that when one man gets ahead it must necessarily be at some one else's expense.

But the truth is the very opposite. The progress of society is like that of a great party of men who are trying to make their way over a rough, untrodden road, in some wilderness of the West. Such a party gets along most successfully when every man in it is allowed to use his legs in the best way he can, and to get along as fast as he can. Every man who is ahead of another has to make a better road for him; every stone or stick he knocks out of his way makes a smoother road for all who are to follow, and thus while those who are ahead enjoy an advantage over their fellows, those who are behind have the advantage of a better road.

Now the theory that one man should not be allowed to get ahead of another would lead to the practice of tying such a party of men together, both by their hands and feet, so that one could step only when another did.

Another form of the same fallacy is seen in the current notion that one man is worse off because others accumulate immense fortunes. I have shown abundantly that no man can accumulate a fortune except by benefiting his fellow-men, and especially the laborer, by much more than the whole value of the fortune. Nor is this all. I have shown that after his fortune is acquired he cannot do much with it except employ it for the benefit of his fellow-men.

I have written these talks because the singular spectacle was presented to me of a large body of men organizing and contributing money to do themselves all the injury they well could. What suffering they have thus caused themselves you all know. What privation the poor will endure next winter in consequence of the agitation thus brought about you will see when next winter comes. I hope you will not then forget the cause of the distress.

XX.
CONCLUSION.

I now invite the reader's courteous attention to some general thoughts about the subject we have been discussing. I do not profess to have solved the labor problem; I do not think it is to be solved on any system, or by any theory, which can be laid down either by a man or a body of men. I am an optimist to this extent: It seems to me that the system on which men have gradually been led to work in unison by merely following the course dictated by circumstances in each individual case works better than any which human ingenuity could have contrived. Studying the effect of governmental interference in the past we find that whenever it was dictated by any economic theory it retarded rather than promoted progress. We now look back with wonder upon the unwise policy of the Spanish government consequent upon the discovery of America. Yet it was dictated by the commercial theories which then moved the world, though individuals never acted on them. We now see very clearly that the policy to which individuals were led merely by following their own interests, and acting as circumstance dictated, was wiser, and tended more to the public good, than any system which had received the sanction of government.

I think the same thing is true at the present time. Our posterity of a century or two hence will ask with wonder how the people of the United States in this nineteenth century could have believed, in the face of reason and facts, that the condition of the laborer would be improved by a policy designed to make everything necessary to his comfort scarce and dear, by levying protective tariffs upon everything he might import from foreign countries, by discouraging him from building ships and from engaging in many other forms of industry, and by persuading him to produce as few of the necessaries of life as possible.

As in the past the stern logic of facts has proved stronger than any theories of philosophers or people, so I think it will be in the future. The inherent tendency of the individual to do what is for his own good, will, in the long run, overpower all other tendencies. This will lead to the very best results, because, when every individual does what is best for himself the whole community will be doing what is best for the whole community.

I by no means claim that neither legislation nor regulation will enter as factors into the result. Our courts of law will see that no man is allowed to pursue his own selfish good at the expense of others, without rendering them a full equivalent for all he takes from them, and that corporations shall treat all men alike. We are approaching a new state of things, which will need new laws. Each new law framed to meet an evident emergency will probably be a wise law; if it is unwise that fact will soon be found out and the law will be changed.

If, then, I hold that the logic of events is wiser than the philosophy of men, why have I penned these chapters? I reply, to set forth that aspect of the question which seems most in need of being set forth. Our natural progress towards a healthy social state is retarded by the prevalence of false theories which permeate society and control legislation. The constant tendency towards unwise legislation is the greatest difficulty society now has to encounter. It forms the only basis on which the so-called Manchester School of Political Economy can now rest, and the only obstacle to the introduction into legislation of those more liberal and philanthropic ideas which so many of our philosophers are disseminating.

Is it possible to get through Congress any legislation on the labor problem which will not be inimical to the interest of laborers? Judging from the past, the outlook is not encouraging. Let us add one more to the instances already given of unsound theories in legislation.

Why have we not American shipping and American ship-building? Because our laws throw obstacles in the way of an American citizen building a ship, or sailing one he has bought abroad under the American flag. If Congress should merely repeal all laws which in any way abridge the right of citizens of the United States to import all the material and machinery needed to build ships with, and all laws which in any manner restrict them in the purchase of ships already built, we should in a few years have an American mercantile marine of respectable proportions. Please remember that no positive legislation is needed for this purpose, all we need is the repeal of adverse legislation.

The question whether state regulation of great organizations will be a feature of our coming policy turns on this very point. If we can ever get a system of legislation which shall be based on business principles and not on erroneous social theories, we may expect a continual enlargement of the functions of the state. There are many things which the state would do better than any corporation, could we only have it embody the wisdom of the nation.

The careful reader of this little book will see that it is written entirely from the point of view of the interests of laborers. I have nowhere considered the interests, and seldom the rights, of capitalists and employers. I look forward to the time when no one will have to labor more than eight hours a day to make a living. This time will come when a few more improvements are made in machinery, and when every boy shall be trained in doing something useful to his fellows, and be allowed the same rights whether he is or is not a member of a labor organization. It would approach very rapidly could we once get rid of the theory that plenty and cheapness are evils, and high prices the only good.

Notwithstanding my optimistic views, I am not unmindful of the dark side of the case. The darkest feature of all is that the maximum of discontent has come with the maximum of prosperity among laborers. Never before could the industrious laborer make a living so easily as he can to-day, never before could he spend so much time and money in disseminating his views, and never has there been so much organized discontent the world over. I know it is sometimes said that the laborer is no better off for modern improvements in production, but this statement is so absurdly contrary to facts which anybody can know by merely opening his eyes and studying, that it can hardly be characterized as otherwise than reckless. When I walk out in the city of Washington on a Sunday afternoon I find the public parks and streets swarming with the children and wives of laborers, every one of them dressed in a style which, when I was a boy, was possible only to the rich. I suppose the same to be true in all our cities.

In saying this I do not claim that the condition of everybody is improved. There are in every community large numbers of people who have not been trained to follow any special pursuit, whose wants are very few and simple, who are willing to go barefoot in summer and eat the cheapest food the year round, who want nothing but a hovel to shelter them, and nothing but rags to clothe them, and who will do just what is necessary to supply these simple wants, and nothing more. Of course, such people would never be any better off under any conditions that we could devise. They stay behind simply because they do not want to take the trouble to go ahead. It is useless to smooth the road before them because they will not walk upon it, no matter how smooth we make it.

A pessimist might claim that progress which results only in discontent is an evil; that the very fact of the laborer being discontented with his improved condition shows that it has improved too rapidly, that a social cataclysm is imminent which will once more reduce him to the state of coarse bread, rags, and a hovel, which was his lot in times past. All I can say in reply is, that I hope for the best.

THE END.

The Codes Of Hammurabi And Moses
W. W. Davies

QTY

The discovery of the Hammurabi Code is one of the greatest achievements of archaeology, and is of paramount interest, not only to the student of the Bible, but also to all those interested in ancient history...

Religion   **ISBN:** *1-59462-338-4*   **Pages:132**
MSRP $12.95

The Theory of Moral Sentiments
Adam Smith

QTY

This work from 1749. contains original theories of conscience amd moral judgment and it is the foundation for systemof morals.

Philosophy   **ISBN:** *1-59462-777-0*   **Pages:536**
MSRP $19.95

Jessica's First Prayer
Hesba Stretton

QTY

In a screened and secluded corner of one of the many railway-bridges which span the streets of London there could be seen a few years ago, from five o'clock every morning until half past eight, a tidily set-out coffee-stall, consisting of a trestle and board, upon which stood two large tin cans, with a small fire of charcoal burning under each so as to keep the coffee boiling during the early hours of the morning when the work-people were thronging into the city on their way to their daily toil...

Pages:84

Childrens   **ISBN:** *1-59462-373-2*   **MSRP $9.95**

My Life and Work
Henry Ford

QTY

Henry Ford revolutionized the world with his implementation of mass production for the Model T automobile. Gain valuable business insight into his life and work with his own auto-biography... "We have only started on our development of our country we have not as yet, with all our talk of wonderful progress, done more than scratch the surface. The progress has been wonderful enough but..."

Pages:300

Biographies/   **ISBN:** *1-59462-198-5*   **MSRP $21.95**

www.bookjungle.com *email: sales@bookjungle.com fax: 630-214-0564 mail: Book Jungle PO Box 2226 Champaign, IL 61825*

The Art of Cross-Examination
Francis Wellman

QTY

I presume it is the experience of every author, after his first book is published upon an important subject, to be almost overwhelmed with a wealth of ideas and illustrations which could readily have been included in his book, and which to his own mind, at least, seem to make a second edition inevitable. Such certainly was the case with me; and when the first edition had reached its sixth impression in five months, I rejoiced to learn that it seemed to my publishers that the book had met with a sufficiently favorable reception to justify a second and considerably enlarged edition. ..

Pages:412

Reference   **ISBN:** *1-59462-647-2*   *MSRP $19.95*

On the Duty of Civil Disobedience
Henry David Thoreau

QTY

Thoreau wrote his famous essay, On the Duty of Civil Disobedience, as a protest against an unjust but popular war and the immoral but popular institution of slave-owning. He did more than write—he declined to pay his taxes, and was hauled off to gaol in consequence. Who can say how much this refusal of his hastened the end of the war and of slavery ?

Law   **ISBN:** *1-59462-747-9*   **Pages:48**

MSRP $7.45

Dream Psychology Psychoanalysis for Beginners
Sigmund Freud

QTY

Sigmund Freud, born Sigismund Schlomo Freud (May 6, 1856 - September 23, 1939), was a Jewish-Austrian neurologist and psychiatrist who co-founded the psychoanalytic school of psychology. Freud is best known for his theories of the unconscious mind, especially involving the mechanism of repression; his redefinition of sexual desire as mobile and directed towards a wide variety of objects; and his therapeutic techniques, especially his understanding of transference in the therapeutic relationship and the presumed value of dreams as sources of insight into unconscious desires.

Pages:196

Psychology   **ISBN:** *1-59462-905-6*   *MSRP $15.45*

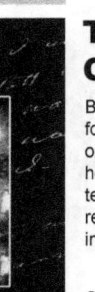

The Miracle of Right Thought
Orison Swett Marden

QTY

Believe with all of your heart that you will do what you were made to do. When the mind has once formed the habit of holding cheerful, happy, prosperous pictures, it will not be easy to form the opposite habit. It does not matter how improbable or how far away this realization may see, or how dark the prospects may be, if we visualize them as best we can, as vividly as possible, hold tenaciously to them and vigorously struggle to attain them, they will gradually become actualized, realized in the life. But a desire, a longing without endeavor, a yearning abandoned or held indifferently will vanish without realization.

Pages:360

Self Help   **ISBN:** *1-59462-644-8*   *MSRP $25.45*

www.bookjungle.com *email: sales@bookjungle.com fax: 630-214-0564 mail: Book Jungle PO Box 2226 Champaign, IL 61825*

QTY

The Rosicrucian Cosmo-Conception Mystic Christianity *by Max Heindel* ISBN: *1-59462-188-8* **$38.95**
The Rosicrucian Cosmo-conception is not dogmatic, neither does it appeal to any other authority than the reason of the student. It is: not controversial, but is: sent forth in the, hope that it may help to clear... New Age/Religion Pages 646

Abandonment To Divine Providence *by Jean-Pierre de Caussade* ISBN: *1-59462-228-0* **$25.95**
"The Rev. Jean Pierre de Caussade was one of the most remarkable spiritual writers of the Society of Jesus in France in the 18th Century. His death took place at Toulouse in 1751. His works have gone through many editions and have been republished... Inspirational/Religion Pages 400

Mental Chemistry *by Charles Haanel* ISBN: *1-59462-192-6* **$23.95**
Mental Chemistry allows the change of material conditions by combining and appropriately utilizing the power of the mind. Much like applied chemistry creates something new and unique out of careful combinations of chemicals the mastery of mental chemistry... New Age Pages 354

The Letters of Robert Browning and Elizabeth Barret Barrett 1845-1846 vol II ISBN: *1-59462-193-4* **$35.95**
by Robert Browning and Elizabeth Barrett Biographies Pages 596

Gleanings In Genesis (volume I) *by Arthur W. Pink* ISBN: *1-59462-130-6* **$27.45**
Appropriately has Genesis been termed "the seed plot of the Bible" for in it we have, in germ form, almost all of the great doctrines which are afterwards fully developed in the books of Scripture which follow... Religion/Inspirational Pages 420

The Master Key *by L. W. de Laurence* ISBN: *1-59462-001-6* **$30.95**
In no branch of human knowledge has there been a more lively increase of the spirit of research during the past few years than in the study of Psychology, Concentration and Mental Discipline. The requests for authentic lessons in Thought Control, Mental Discipline and... New Age/Business Pages 422

The Lesser Key Of Solomon Goetia *by L. W. de Laurence* ISBN: *1-59462-092-X* **$9.95**
This translation of the first book of the "Lernegton" which is now for the first time made accessible to students of Talismanic Magic was done, after careful collation and edition, from numerous Ancient Manuscripts in Hebrew, Latin, and French... New Age/Occult Pages 92

Rubaiyat Of Omar Khayyam *by Edward Fitzgerald* ISBN:*1-59462-332-5* **$13.95**
Edward Fitzgerald, whom the world has already learned, in spite of his own efforts to remain within the shadow of anonymity, to look upon as one of the rarest poets of the century, was born at Bredfield, in Suffolk, on the 31st of March, 1809. He was the third son of John Purcell... Music Pages 172

Ancient Law *by Henry Maine* ISBN: *1-59462-128-4* **$29.95**
The chief object of the following pages is to indicate some of the earliest ideas of mankind, as they are reflected in Ancient Law, and to point out the relation of those ideas to modern thought. Religion/History Pages 452

Far-Away Stories *by William J. Locke* ISBN: *1-59462-129-2* **$19.45**
"Good wine needs no bush, but a collection of mixed vintages does. And this book is just such a collection. Some of the stories I do not want to remain buried for ever in the museum files of dead magazine-numbers an author's not unpardonable vanity..." Fiction Pages 272

Life of David Crockett *by David Crockett* ISBN: *1-59462-250-7* **$27.45**
"Colonel David Crockett was one of the most remarkable men of the times in which he lived. Born in humble life, but gifted with a strong will, an indomitable courage, and unremitting perseverance... Biographies/New Age Pages 424

Lip-Reading *by Edward Nitchie* ISBN: *1-59462-206-X* **$25.95**
Edward B. Nitchie, founder of the New York School for the Hard of Hearing, now the Nitchie School of Lip-Reading, Inc, wrote "LIP-READING Principles and Practice". The development and perfecting of this meritorious work on lip-reading was an undertaking... How-to Pages 400

A Handbook of Suggestive Therapeutics, Applied Hypnotism, Psychic Science ISBN: *1-59462-214-0* **$24.95**
by Henry Munro Health/New Age/Health/Self-help Pages 376

A Doll's House: and Two Other Plays *by Henrik Ibsen* ISBN: *1-59462-112-8* **$19.95**
Henrik Ibsen created this classic when in revolutionary 1848 Rome. Introducing some striking concepts in playwriting for the realist genre, this play has been studied the world over. Fiction/Classics/Plays 308

The Light of Asia *by sir Edwin Arnold* ISBN: *1-59462-204-3* **$13.95**
In this poetic masterpiece, Edwin Arnold describes the life and teachings of Buddha. The man who was to become known as Buddha to the world was born as Prince Gautama of India but he rejected the worldly riches and abandoned the reigns of power when... Religion/History/Biographies Pages 170

The Complete Works of Guy de Maupassant *by Guy de Maupassant* ISBN: *1-59462-157-8* **$16.95**
"For days and days, nights and nights, I had dreamed of that first kiss which was to consecrate our engagement, and I knew not on what spot I should put my lips..." Fiction/Classics Pages 240

The Art of Cross-Examination *by Francis L. Wellman* ISBN: *1-59462-309-0* **$26.95**
Written by a renowned trial lawyer, Wellman imparts his experience and uses case studies to explain how to use psychology to extract desired information through questioning. How-to/Science/Reference Pages 408

Answered or Unanswered? *by Louisa Vaughan* ISBN: *1-59462-248-5* **$10.95**
Miracles of Faith in China Religion Pages 112

The Edinburgh Lectures on Mental Science (1909) *by Thomas* ISBN: *1-59462-008-3* **$11.95**
This book contains the substance of a course of lectures recently given by the writer in the Queen Street Hall, Edinburgh. Its purpose is to indicate the Natural Principles governing the relation between Mental Action and Material Conditions... New Age/Psychology Pages 148

Ayesha *by H. Rider Haggard* ISBN: *1-59462-301-5* **$24.95**
Verily and indeed it is the unexpected that happens! Probably if there was one person upon the earth from whom the Editor of this, and of a certain previous history, did not expect to hear again... Classics Pages 380

Ayala's Angel *by Anthony Trollope* ISBN: *1-59462-352-X* **$29.95**
The two girls were both pretty, but Lucy who was twenty-one who supposed to be simple and comparatively unattractive, whereas Ayala was credited, as her Bombwhat romantic name might show, with poetic charm and a taste for romance. Ayala when her father died was nineteen... Fiction Pages 484

The American Commonwealth *by James Bryce* ISBN: *1-59462-286-8* **$34.45**
An interpretation of American democratic political theory. It examines political mechanics and society from the perspective of Scotsman James Bryce Politics Pages 572

Stories of the Pilgrims *by Margaret P. Pumphrey* ISBN: *1-59462-116-0* **$17.95**
This book explores pilgrims religious oppression in England as well as their escape to Holland and eventual crossing to America on the Mayflower, and their early days in New England... History Pages 268

www.bookjungle.com *email: sales@bookjungle.com fax: 630-214-0564 mail: Book Jungle PO Box 2226 Champaign, IL 61825*

QTY

The Fasting Cure *by Sinclair Upton* ISBN: *1-59462-222-1* **$13.95**
In the Cosmopolitan Magazine for May, 1910, and in the Contemporary Review (London) for April, 1910, I published an article dealing with my experiences in fasting. I have written a great many magazine articles, but never one which attracted so much attention... New Age/Self Help/Health Pages 164

Hebrew Astrology *by Sepharial* ISBN: *1-59462-308-2* **$13.45**
In these days of advanced thinking it is a matter of common observation that we have left many of the old landmarks behind and that we are now pressing forward to greater heights and to a wider horizon than that which represented the mind-content of our progenitors... Astrology Pages 144

Thought Vibration or The Law of Attraction in the Thought World ISBN: *1-59462-127-6* **$12.95**
by William Walker Atkinson Psychology/Religion Pages 144

Optimism *by Helen Keller* ISBN: *1-59462-108-X* **$15.95**
Helen Keller was blind, deaf, and mute since 19 months old, yet famously learned how to overcome these handicaps, communicate with the world, and spread her lectures promoting optimism. An inspiring read for everyone... Biographies/Inspirational Pages 84

Sara Crewe *by Frances Burnett* ISBN: *1-59462-360-0* **$9.45**
In the first place, Miss Minchin lived in London. Her home was a large, dull, tall one, in a large, dull square, where all the houses were alike, and all the sparrows were alike, and where all the door-knockers made the same heavy sound... Childrens/Classic Pages 88

The Autobiography of Benjamin Franklin *by Benjamin Franklin* ISBN: *1-59462-135-7* **$24.95**
The Autobiography of Benjamin Franklin has probably been more extensively read than any other American historical work, and no other book of its kind has had such ups and downs of fortune. Franklin lived for many years in England, where he was agent... Biographies/History Pages 332

Name	
Email	
Telephone	
Address	
City, State ZIP	

☐ **Credit Card**   ☐ **Check / Money Order**

Credit Card Number	
Expiration Date	
Signature	

Please Mail to: Book Jungle
PO Box 2226
Champaign, IL 61825
or Fax to: 630-214-0564

ORDERING INFORMATION
web*: www.bookjungle.com*
email*: sales@bookjungle.com*
fax*: 630-214-0564*
mail*: Book Jungle PO Box 2226 Champaign, IL 61825*
or PayPal *to sales@bookjungle.com*

Please contact us for bulk discounts

DIRECT-ORDER TERMS
20% Discount if You Order Two or More Books
Free Domestic Shipping!
Accepted: Master Card, Visa, Discover, American Express

www.ingramcontent.com/pod-product-compliance
Lightning Source LLC
Chambersburg PA
CBHW082016170626
46817CB00009B/3114